THE MOST BEAUTIFUL NIGHT OF THE SOUL

THE MOST BEAUTIFUL NIGHT OF THE SOUL

More Stories from the Middle East and Beyond

Sándor Jászberényi

Translated from the Hungarian by Paul Olchváry

SPEAKING TIGER

Speaking Tiger Books LLP
4381/4, Ansari Road, Daryaganj
New Delhi - 110002

First published in Hungarian in 2016 by Pesti Kalligram Kft., Budapest.

Portions of this book have appeared in *AGNI Online*, *Tablet*, *Guernica*, and the *Irish Times.*

First published in English in the US by New Europe Books 2019
First published in the Indian subcontinent by Speaking Tiger Books 2020

ISBN: 978-93-89692-06-8
eISBN: 978-93-89692-07-5

10 9 8 7 6 5 4 3 2 1

Printed at Sapra Bothers, Noida. U.P.

Contents

To all the dead I know

The Emperors of Existence

It was dawn, tepid, starless. The sky above Cairo was a bloody gob of spit. We'd gotten into a scrap on the street over some nonsense. For example, who should have the last gulp of whiskey from the last bottle. I'd raised that bottle out of the plastic bag to my mouth when Sanders muttered something. A moment later I head-butted the pavement.

He was on top of me at once. He knelt on my chest, his sweat-soaked shirt touching my skin. He began beating my head against the asphalt in a measured beat. Blood flowed from my mouth. I became fucking nervous. With my free hand I reached toward my pocket. I was looking for the knife so I could stab the scumbag. It was a reflex action, but I might have thought about it first: I myself had left the knife on the table earlier, so that if anything happened outside, the cops wouldn't find it on me.

In post-revolution Egypt it didn't take much to be locked up without charge. One switchblade was enough.

All I achieved by digging through my pocket was that my loose change scattered about.

Sanders didn't let up. His eyes were bloodshot. I was certain he would kill me. My head banged on the pavement five times before I managed to kick him off me. He flew four metres, smashing against the side of a nearby kiosk with a loud thud.

He sprang to his feet immediately. I stood up, too. He tried knocking me to the ground again, but this time I was ready. I stepped out in front of him, hooked a foot between his legs, and planted a fist, hard, on the nape of his neck.

I should kill him, I thought, turning after him. *Why can't he fucking hold his liquor?*

The evening began when he called me saying he wanted to celebrate. His contract had been extended. It was now beyond a doubt that he would remain the foreign affairs editor.

"You'll have some work out of this for a while, too," he said, and I murmured acquiescently.

We agreed to meet in Zamalek, at Deals.

We'd gotten through a few long weeks. I'd reported from Khan Yunis, in the Gaza Strip, on the bombings, and he took over after two weeks. We both saw lots of shit.

At first I didn't want to go anywhere. It would be best not to blow all the money I'd earned. But then I saw online that Rebecca had gone out partying. She'd dropped off the kid at someone's place.

It's not good if you're a man and alone when others are fucking your kid's mother. I got on my leather jacket and left. I took a cab all the way down the Corniche, along the Nile. The wind was hot; my shirt stuck immediately to my skin. After we drove off the 6th October Bridge, I had the cab stop in front of the American bookstore and went from there on foot to the bar, where Sanders was waiting.

It was an American-style sports bar, with big screens on the walls. An Arab guy in a white shirt was standing out front. When I told him that someone was waiting for me inside, he let me in.

Sanders was sitting right by the entrance at a round table. Before him were four daiquiris in goblets, and he was picking out the little, orange parasols. He meticulously closed each of them and lined them up beside the ashtray.

"So, what's up, motherfucker?" he said on seeing me.

"Everything's okay."

I sat down beside him, downed one of the daiquiris, and lit a cigarette.

"You came back through the tunnel, right?" Sanders asked.

"Yep."

"Lucky fuckin' devil."

"I'm simply better than you, dog."

He too downed a daiquiri, and then raised the next glass. I did the same.

"Those pictures of that school hit by a rocket weren't shit, I'll say."

During the Israeli offensive a rocket had struck a school in Gaza. The whole building caved in, all the cars out front burned to a crisp, and the flames even bent the jungle gyms in the school playground. There were spots of blood and abandoned toys all over the pavement. Hamas hadn't let anyone leave the building. It was a horrible sight.

"Whose dead dog was that in the picture?

"The caretaker's."

"Cool. Readers love that sort of thing."

"Dead dogs?"

"Nothing shows the horrors of the conflict more than a dead little dog."

"Fuck that."

"It's not I who said that, but the editor-in-chief."

"That woman is a stupid moron."

"Yeah, she doesn't get fucked like she should."

"Well, you're the section chief, so it would be your responsibility."

"I don't fuck hairy women."

We fell silent. Sanders ordered four more daiquiris. I thought of the editor-in-chief. I'd seen her just once. She was a short, black-haired, Lebanese Christian chick, with thick black knots of hair on her hands.

The waiter emerged with the new daiquiris, put them one by one on the table, and brought a bowl of popcorn, too. Sanders stuffed his face with popcorn, picked the parasols out of the goblets, lined them up yet again, and said:

"We are the emperors of existence."

"We are indeed."

"We've got lives of gold."

"That's right."

"But seriously now. We make more money than we could possibly fucking blow in this city."

"You can fucking blow anything."

"Sure, if you buy a TV, a car, or something like that. But we don't buy things like that."

"We sure don't."

"That's what I'm saying. We're the emperors of existence."

We each downed another one.

"Tonight we'll celebrate, Dan, my boy. We'll let off some steam."

"Okay."

"We've worked our asses off."

"Yeah. Will we go out to Ma'adi?"

"We can go, but first we'll drop by at Kim's, since she's having a party in our honor."

"When are we leaving?"

"We should wait for someone. This character named Elih, from New York. A Jewish kid who came to save the world."

"Great."

We downed one more round of drinks before the guy arrived. He spoke on and on about how much he respects us. He held an entire little presentation about what an important thing war reporting is and, once he finished, he paid the whole bill.

Kim was Sanders's Asian woman, from Washington, DC. She was one lovely little gal, short, with a good figure and almond-shaped eyes. She worked at American Relief. According to Sanders, she fucked as if everything was happening for the last time ever. She really wanted to be chummy with me. She thought I was Sanders's only close friend.

Before the three of us—Sanders, Elih, and I—headed over to Kim's party, we stopped in at Drinkies, on 26th July Street, and bought two bottles of Auld Stag whisky. The clerk put the liquor in black plastic bags. Right in front of the store we began taking swigs from one of the bottles. Auld Stag is the only whisky in Egypt certain not to make you go blind. It tastes like paint thinner.

We'd had half the bottle by the time we got to Kim's rented flat. Elih got drunk in no time, and his New York Jewish pride burst forth. He began to sing, loudly, "*Hevenu shalom Aleichem*," or something of the sort. Sanders and I looked at each other.

"He's your fellow countryman," I said, "so *you* tell him."

"Fuck that."

It seemed there wouldn't be a problem, that he'd stop on his own, but we were wrong. After every swig of liquor came more Jewish songs, including the Israeli national anthem. Finally Sanders stopped and took the bottle from the kid's hand.

"Listen here, for fuck's sake, you finish this motherfucking fast."

"What?"

"The singing."

"Are you two anti-Semitic?"

"No, for fuck's sake, we just want to stay alive."

"You're anti-Semitic."

"No, for fuck's sake, we're in Cairo. They don't like Jews around here. I'm Jewish, too. And him, he's Hungarian. That's almost the same."

"Self-hating Jews," said Elih, and he sang no more.

The woman lived on the top floor of a tower block, in a huge apartment with the other American Relief staff. We were in the most important part of Zamalek. The building had a concierge, in a uniform and service cap, who allowed us to proceed to the elevators' brass doors.

In the elevator Sanders grinned at me. "We're the emperors of existence," he said. Elih leaned up against the wall. A drunken sweat had soaked through his shirt, and he was deathly pale. As soon as we reached the top floor, we heard the sounds of the party. Soul music filtered out from behind a thick, walnut door. Sanders led the way. Inside, some thirty people were chatting away in one large space, glasses in their hands. Kim, in a backless evening dress, headed toward us with a big smile.

"David, hey."

"Hey, baby," said Sanders, planting two kisses on her face. "How's your dad?"

"He's well. Strong as an ox. Bearing the chemo."

"Danny. I'm happy you came."

"I'm happy you invited me."

I turned around. Elih was nowhere to be seen. I looked around the room and caught sight of him sitting on one of the gray couches, his head on his knees.

"Can I have everyone's attention for a moment?" Kim called out.

"I'd like you to be extra nice to these two gentlemen. They just got back from the Gaza Strip. And just today, David Sanders was named foreign affairs editor of the *Egypt Independent.*"

Several people applauded.

"You see?" said Sanders, turning to me with a grin. "Like I said, we're the emperors of existence. Come on, let's go chew on a bit of khat."

We went back to the balcony, where a kilo of green khat leaves was lying on a white plastic table. Yemeni dealers home-delivered them to Zamalek. Five people were sitting around the table, Americans. Each one had a stuffed cheek.

Sanders stepped over, grabbed a big handful of leaves, turned to me, pressed a helping into my hand, and crammed the rest into his cheek. He went off to get two glasses too, which we filled with whisky as chasers.

"I've got to go chew the fat with Kim," he grumbled. "Stay here meanwhile."

"Okay."

I sat down in one of the chairs and chewed away at the khat. My saliva got unbearably sour, so I watered it down with whisky.

"Hello," said a woman next to me. She smiled.

"Hello."

She was around twenty, with short hair and buck teeth.

"So you're the war correspondent."

"Uh-huh."

"I'd like to do that, too."

"Terrific."

"You could give me a couple of tips."

"Now?"

"No, I'd give you my number."

"Okay."

We fell silent.

"I'm called Alba, and I'm in my final year at the American University here in Cairo, majoring in Middle Eastern politics."

She reached out her hand.

"I'm drunk."

She laughed politely. She looked me over. I was certain that if I wanted, I could fuck her.

"I love this song," she said. "Don't you want to dance?"

It was Adele Cure's rendition of "Lovesong." I could feel the khat taking effect.

"I need to go to the bathroom," I said, and stood up. I need to throw up whenever I hear any version of this song.

I fought my way through the crowd. The bathroom was enormous, with a Jacuzzi and a lifesize mirror. I spit all the khat into the toilet and stood before the mirror. My pupils had become as narrow as could be, and I was bathing in sweat.

I imagined that just then someone was screwing my kid's mother. I could see the dude's mug right in front of me.

"We're the emperors of existence," I said. With full force I punched the tile wall. My fist tore open, blood flowed.

I got back out to see Sanders in a shoving match with a big black guy.

"I don't give a shit who you are, for fuck's sake, but you can't talk that way with Kim."

I understood everything. Making my way slowly around them, I looked for an empty beer bottle, smashed it against the wall, and stepped up beside Sanders.

"Think twice about what you're doing," I told the guy. A smug grin came over Sanders's face.

"And who are you?"

"I'm no one. The question is, who he is."

"I don't care who he is."

"But you'd do well to care."

"And why's that?"

"Because it doesn't fucking matter to him."

"Me neither."

"So you won't stop, either, until he's on the ground and bleeding."

"No."

"Think twice about what you've got to lose, though, because he doesn't have a thing in the whole world. Besides, it's two of us on you."

"Cut it out, all of you," said Kim. "Stop it and go away."

Her tears had smeared her makeup.

"Let's get going," I told Sanders, and began pulling him out of the crowd. He didn't resist.

"What the fuck was that?" I asked in the elevator.

"Kim got on my case again about us moving together and building a relationship."

"And you?"

"People get bored of each other and die."

"Ah. What about Elih? We left him up there."

"Fuck him. Let's go to Ma'adi."

"Let's."

"We're the emperors of existence."

"That, we are."

We went all the way down 26th July Street and meanwhile opened the second bottle of whisky. Sanders mumbled something and was on top of me already.

I should kill him, I thought, and leapt after him. He was just standing back up. I planted a fist in his face, full force. He fell back to the ground.

"Die!" I shouted, hitting his head.

"This is for not holding your liquor."

"This is for the fucking bombed-out school."

"This is for my kid being on his own."

"This is for the fucking work we do."

Blood poured from his nose, and his eyebrows tore open.

"Give up, for fuck's sake, 'cause I'll kill you."

He didn't give up. That's the type of guy he was, not the sort to surrender as long as he had a working bone in his body. He reached for my head. I punched him again, full force, at which he broke out laughing. Hysterical laughing drowned out increasingly by a choking cough that echoed through the street. I, too, began to laugh.

"My father died," he said, taking out a handkerchief and dabbing his face.

Beef Tongue

The Estoril is an elegant old, family-run restaurant in downtown Cairo. The wood-paneled walls include illustrations evoking Greek mythology, and the tablecloths are checkered. The Estoril is a restaurant, not a bar, but it does have a liquor license as well. Those who venture in only to drink can sit down at the lacquered bar. The drinks always include some snack—dry Arab bread, curd cheese with olive oil and arugula—and this makes the Estoril quite popular among social drinkers. But the restaurant's chief attraction is undeniably its kitchen, where the owner himself, along with his family, prepare the dishes. On weekends it's almost impossible to find a table, and at such times the place fills up with liberals and foreigners who, under the colonial-era chandeliers, drink red wine with boiled beef tongue, which is the house specialty. It is served with horseradish sauce and boiled until it is soft enough to cut with a fork.

"I simply can't believe that they've already announced the position," said Kaufmann, a black-haired man in his mid-thirties, passing his eyes over those at the table. Three others were sitting there, two men and one woman. They had just finished supper. The two other men, Yakov and Joe, were likewise freelance journalists in Cairo, and the woman was Martha Lindsey, who had been John Hartmann's girlfriend.

Two weeks earlier Hartmann had been shot dead by a unit of the Syrian Liberation Front. They had opened fire accidentally on the car John was in, but by the time they realized, everyone inside was dead. Thomson Reuters officially mourned his loss as one of its own. The three men had previously gone to the Estoril often with John and Martha, but this was the group's first time there since the incident. Kaufmann had reserved the table and placed the order in advance.

"I can't believe it," he repeated.

"You can't be serious," replied Joe. "Why, that really is pretty tasteless."

"That, it is. But I'll wait and see how they'll manage to find an authority of John's caliber," said Yakov.

"I don't even understand this," said Martha, a tear coming into her eye. "I wrote to his editor asking them to wait. At least until I get back to London to pack his things."

"And what was the reply?"

"That the demand for news is enormous, and the company cannot allow itself to wait."

"Animals," said Yakov. "But what could you expect from a multinational anyway?"

"How are you, Martha?" asked Kaufmann. "You haven't even touched your supper." The beef tongue lay untouched on her plate.

"Good," replied Martha, sniffling. "Only that I can't sleep, and I'm drinking too much." Kaufmann looked over Martha. She was pale and the tears had smeared her makeup, but even so, she was a decidedly lovely blonde.

"I figure that's completely normal in the given circumstances," said Yakov.

"I can't square everyday life, either, with John having been killed."

"I think none of us can."

They ordered a bottle of ouzo, and the waiter delivered it with a jug of water.

"To John," said Kaufmann, raising his glass high. The others followed his example.

"Do you all remember the time he managed to land an interview in the Gaza Strip with the head of Islamic Jihad? For three years a picture hadn't even appeared of the character, but John was able to take one."

"He was a fucking good reporter," said Yakov.

"And a good friend," said Joe. "When I was robbed in Juba, in South Sudan, he was the first to give me a phone call and send me money. He could always be counted on."

"He loved you boys," said Martha. "He was the best man I knew."

"Believe me, John loved you more than anyone in the world. You were his love, and he could imagine his life only with you. I remember that it was because he wanted to get home on time to you that he avoided late-night partying with the boys. But, God, how he could hold his liquor! He could drink as much as a whole football team."

"Let's drink to that!" cried out Kaufmann, refilling the glasses. "To John, whom we could party with."

They drank, and then fell silent for a while.

"And you, Martha," asked Yakov, "what will you do now?"

"I think I'll go home to my mother, in London. After all, I moved here to Cairo because of John, and now that he's died, there's no sense in my staying. Even so, it is pretty horrible going back to the flat where his things are. I'm always expecting him to show up. I've got no business in Cairo without John."

"I understand you completely," said Kaufmann. "This city is no place for a single woman."

"That's for sure," said Joe. "Even Yakov was robbed!"

"My God, Yakov, what happened?" asked Martha.

"It's nothing. Last week the cops confiscated my camera."

"What kind of machine was it?" asked Kaufmann.

"A Canon 5D. They took everything. The camera, the lenses, everything. For four hours straight I sat at a police station trying to prove that I'm not a spy."

"And what are you taking photos with now?"

"Nothing. I'm saving up for a new camera," he said. His face clouded over. "Five thousand dollars is no little money."

"My poor thing," said the woman, caressing the man's hand.

"It's nothing."

"Do you guys remember when last year all three of us were nearly arrested on Mohammed Mahmoud Street, and it was John who talked them into letting us go?" asked Kaufmann, refilling the glasses.

"Maybe they wouldn't have taken my camera if he'd been there," said Yakov.

"If only he was here with us."

"To John."

They drank again. Kaufmann had not skimped in filling the glasses. There was hardly any ouzo left in the bottle. By now all of them felt the alcohol. The woman's face turned red.

"Say, Martha, did they take John home?" asked Joe. "I mean, you know, the funeral."

"Yes. Medecins Sans Frontieres arranged it. His colleagues in Beirut identified his body."

"Thank God you didn't have to."

"I couldn't have taken that. Even so, it's not at all certain I can. I don't think John . . ." Before she could finish the sentence she burst out crying.

The men fell silent in commiseration.

"You've got to stay strong," Kaufmann finally said. "John would want that, too."

"Yes, I know," said the woman, picking up the red paper napkin from the table and blowing her nose with it.

"Have you talked with his parents?" asked Yakov.

"Yes. His mother is completely devastated. His father is holding his own. They're expecting me next week at their place in London. His dad said he wants to establish some foundation so people can remember what John did. He said he died a hero."

"And he's right about that," said Joe.

"Indeed," said Kaufmann.

"That foundation is a good idea. Worthy of John's spirit."

"This too is why I wanted to talk to you guys. We'll be needing your help if John's father is really to make something of this foundation."

"You know you can count on us," someone said. "We were not only John's friends but also yours."

"Thanks, guys."

The men smiled and the woman smiled back at them.

"It's getting late," said Martha, taking a look at the pink iPhone lying on the table to check the time. It was eleven. They had an hour to go before the start of the curfew. Though in truth no one really bothered with the curfew that was in force across the country. Shops, cafés, and restaurants stayed open, and crowds billowed on the streets.

"The bill, please!" Yakov shouted toward the bar. The large, mustachioed man standing behind it nodded, and then called out in Arabic to one of the waiters, who delivered the bill to their table in a little black leather folder.

"How did you like the supper?" asked the waiter in English.

"It was terrific," sad Kaufmann, the others nodding.

"May I pack up the leftovers for you?"

"Yes, do be so kind," said Yakov.

"It's really not necessary," said Martha. "Really not."

"You've got to eat!" said Kaufmann. "Please take it with you."

The woman acquiesced, whereupon the waiter took the beef tongue to the kitchen, where it was put in a white plastic container. The party paid the bill, everyone chipping in for the cost of the supper, and they all then stepped out the door. Talaat Harb Street was still bustling loudly with life, schlockmeisters offering their wares on both sides of the street and drivers beeping stridently in the crawling traffic.

"You stay strong, now, girl," said Yakov and hugged Martha.

"This is really hard for us, too," someone added, "but you know you can call us anytime."

"Thanks, boys. In John's name, too."

"He was one terrific fellow, and I'm honored to have been his friend," said Kaufmann.

"We are, too," the other two men chimed in.

They went their separate ways. Kaufmann and Martha lived in Heliopolis, so they agreed to catch a cab together. Yakov and Joe politely waited there until the woman, the white plastic bag in her hand, sat into the cab beside Kaufmann.

Quietly they ambled home; they lived only a few apartment buildings away from each other. Joe broke the silence.

"Say, do you think it would be really awkward if I applied for John's position? I'm just really broke, and could damn well use the regular pay."

"Not at all," Yakov replied. "I'd apply, too, if I had a camera."

It was settled.

Later it occurred to Yakov that John had an extra camera in his flat. A Canon 7D. So he wrote the woman a letter spelling out his tragic financial circumstances in some detail, and asked her for the camera.

In the course of the long cab ride Kaufmann persuaded Martha that they should go have a drink somewhere in Heliopolis, and so they did. The one drink became several, and at 2 a.m. he accompanied the woman home, stopping up at the flat to use the washroom. Martha teetered drunkenly in the stairwell, falling into Kaufmann's arms. The man planted his lips on hers, she responded in kind, and they went into Hartmann's flat. As for the plastic bag in which Martha was carrying the boiled beef tongue, they forgot that in the stairwell. By morning it was oozing liquid and swarming with big, black flies.

Winter in the Promised Land

It was winter in Jerusalem, late December. A fine layer of snow covered Golgotha, and winter coats appeared in the Old City. Radiators buzzed in the shops, and hotels adjusted their air conditioners to blow warm air under their five-star arches and fountains.

The smell of burnt cedar pervaded every bit of the Muslim quarter. The breaths of the young men and women on guard duty at checkpoints could be seen in the air. Further off, in the Sinai Desert, pouring rain had caused a mudslide, rendered roads impassable, and washed entire Bedouin villages off the map. But in the foyer of the Waldorf Astoria, by its Art Nouveau clock, there wasn't even a hint of the sudden, stormy weather outside.

I'd just emerged from several long weeks of reporting in the Gaza Strip. On December 23 I'd entered Israel at the Erez Crossing after the Israeli Defense Forces had announced, even to the media, that the situation would further deteriorate and that another military operation could be expected. Compared to Gaza—overcrowded, under a blockade, and in the grips of jihadists—the Waldorf Astoria seemed to me like heaven on earth, what with its velvet-upholstered elevators and spongy mattresses. I sprawled out onto the bed in my room and slept all day.

After waking up I soaked for hours in the two-person bathtub. I kept trying out the lavish selection of shower gels and body lotions that promised to stave off age, wrinkles, and exhaustion.

I couldn't stay here long, I knew. If I wanted to write about the ongoing military operation, I'd have to move to a cheaper accommodation, in Tel Aviv. The army was being secretive about the timing of its offensive. No one knew when the tanks and the air force would be set in motion. Everyone knew the offensive was nearing, though, because homemade rockets were being fired regularly into Israel from Gaza. Five-hundred-dollar Palestinian stone-age rockets were being knocked out of the sky by thirty-thousand-dollar Israeli missiles. And Hamas was not skimping when it came to the number of rockets it shot: the situation for Israel was untenable. On account of the murders in the West Bank and the incoming rockets, the Israeli public demanded blood. Soldiers were ordered to their bases. Everyone was waiting for the order that would set the operation in motion. This could mean days or even weeks, and I meanwhile had to budget my money, unless I wanted to miss out on the hoopla.

On finishing the bath I donned the robe and embroidered slippers, each bearing the hotel logo. I called the front desk to order a pack of cigarettes. Though I still had two packs of Egyptian Cleopatras, I thought I'd smoke normal cigarettes for once, as long as I was here at the Waldorf Astoria at Christmas. *Merry Christmas to me.*

Room service pressed the buzzer within ten minutes. The bellboy delivered the velvety red pack of Marlboros on a little silver tray, with hotel-brand matches, set it on the smoking table, and left. I sat down in the armchair, lit up, and turned on the plasma TV above the bed to be greeted by a commercial in Hebrew, of which I understood not a word. A little boy was sitting across from a robot-dog, speaking to it at length as the dog replied with robotlike barks, and when the boy threw a ball, the dog fetched it. The robot-dog even had a tail, which was wagging and which the camera zeroed in on at the end of the commercial as the boy and other children called out, now in English, "Robodog."

I stepped over to the bar, took out a little bottle of Chivas Regal, poured it into a glass, and drank it down. *Merry Christmas*, I thought, imagining that at this moment my Facebook page was being deluged by tacky, virtual Christmas cards featuring everything from Christmas trees, the baby Jesus in the manger, and sage sentences fished off the Internet about peace and love to big, Christmas-themed shopping specials. It occurred to me that I was close indeed to the little town where, tradition had it, some two thousand years earlier a particular woman had gone into labor on this day and given birth to the world's savior.

Theoretically.

For my part, I'd never perceived so much as a trace of the world having been saved, so Christmas irritated me more than any other holiday. I'd escaped to the Middle East, but in vain: peace specials and last-minute messages of love had followed me even there. Though neither Muslims nor Jews celebrate Christmas, that doesn't keep supermarket chains from heralding the holiest of shopping holidays with discounts.

My phone beeped. I had set it for four o'clock so I could get ready in time for Aviad's arrival at the hotel.

Aviad was my best Israeli source and, of course, also my friend. We knew each other from Budapest. He'd been finishing his compulsory military service in Israel when he fell in love with Éva, a Hungarian Jewish girl vacationing in Tel Aviv. It was a grand love. The moment his service ended he traveled to

Budapest to pursue Éva, who worked as a waitress in the bar I sat in practically every day. He hung out there constantly to be near Éva, and in the meantime the two of us spoke about all sorts of things and became friends. He and Éva went on to have two sons. Early on in their relationship, when Éva finally resolved to move to Israel with him, Aviad returned to the army. Though we hadn't met in years, we kept in touch on Facebook. With his help I was able to enter Israel without having to undergo endlessly unpleasant interrogations on account of all the Arabic stamps in my passport, not even to mention the various pictures taken of me in jihadist circles in the course of my work. With Aviad's intervention I was allowed into Israel without a hassle, and the government press office issued me accreditation, no questions asked. I was issued permits to travel to Gaza, and Aviad told me to stay on, by all means, since war was coming. That's why we had to meet: he'd promised to get a level IV bulletproof vest, which could stop 7.62 armor-piercing ammunition. He said he'd bring it to the hotel at four.

I turned off the phone's snooze mode, got dressed, and went downstairs to the hotel bar. Mahogany plates covered the walls. The bar itself was in the middle of the room, surrounded by round tables with red, damask tablecloths. A large crystal chandelier ensured some light, but the space was characterized more by a pleasant dimness. I sat down at a table, took out a cigarette and lit up. A little while later the waiter appeared: a man of around thirty, with slicked-back black hair and a white shirt, tie, and black vest.

"Merry Christmas, sir."

"Merry Christmas."

"What can I get you?"

"A Budweiser," I replied, referring to the Czech beer.

He nodded and left, and soon reappeared with the beer and a crystal glass, which he put down before me, on the table, and filled.

"Would it bother you if I turned on the TV?" he asked, pointing to the wall, into which a plasma TV was built.

"No, go right ahead."

The waiter returned to the bar and switched on the TV. Again, that commercial with the robot-dog. The dog barked, brought back the ball the boy had thrown, and wagged its tail. But this time what I'd seen before in Hebrew, was in Arabic, though now, too, the call at the end was in English: "Robodog." I drank from my beer and crushed my cigarette. I watched TV. After the commercials, the station showed Ramallah, Bethlehem, and other cities in Palestinian control, Palestinian mass demonstrations, and then the Israeli tank division that had been sent to the vicinity of the Gaza Strip.

The door opened, and in stepped Aviad. He headed toward me with a grin. He wore light brown military trousers and a jacket of the same color. He was beefed up, with at least twenty pounds more muscle than when I'd last seen him.

"So, what's up, you Arab groupie?"

"All's fine and well, you fascist Jew."

I stood. We shook hands and hugged.

"Good to see you, you prick," said Aviad, slapping my back. "I just don't get what the hell you're up to among the Arabs."

"Working. Sit your ass down."

"I can't. I've got two days' leave, got to go home to the kids. It's Christmas."

"You're Jews."

"Explain that to the kid and to the Hungarian gal who's used to a Christmas tree. I'm fine doing lots of things in life, but not telling the two kids that from now on there won't be a Christmas and gifts."

"And Hanukkah?"

"They get gifts then, too. That's how they are."

"At least drink a beer with me. Did you bring the vest?"

"I did. But you won't get away with just that much. Get your stuff together, because you're coming with me. Éva is waiting for you, too."

"I don't want to be in the way. I've got a couple things to do, anyway."

"You won't be in the way."

"When do you want to leave?"

"Now."

"I've got to check out."

"I'll wait for you here."

They lived in Sderot, less than three kilometers from the Gaza Strip. Aviad had been born there; his whole family lived there. He got about in a black, ramshackle Ford Focus. By the time I got out to the hotel parking lot, the engine was running.

"Just toss your stuff onto the back seat," he said.

I opened the rear door. There, on the seat, was a sand-colored, emblemless vest, a Kevlar helmet, and Aviad's military rucksack. Propped up in the child seat was a Tavor TAR-21 assault rifle, its ammunition pouch on the floor. I threw my backpack and laptop bag onto the bulletproof vest, and then sat down in front, beside Aviad.

"No smoking in the car," he said with a grin.

We headed off through snow flurries. In the rush-hour traffic we wormed our way out of the city. For quite a while along the road leading to the main highway I stared at a huge billboard featuring Robodog, recommended for all children for Hanukkah. Aviad turned on the radio: the news, in Hebrew.

"What's being said?" I asked.

"They're firing those rockets all day. All fucking day."

"Did anyone die?"

"No. Those scum don't know how to aim. And we do have the Iron Dome."

"How do Éva and the kids stand it?"

"They get by. She's drilled a lot with them in getting down to the air-raid shelter."

"Are they down there all day?"

"No. Only when the sirens ring out. The Iron Dome is really something. Takes down everything that would fall on the city."

I recalled the pictures I'd taken in Khan Yunis, in the Gaza Strip, of the rocket factory. Aviad was right: in fact the rockets had no guidance systems. They simply had to be fired up and pointed a certain way. They flew as long as their fuel lasted, and then they fell. The explosives they contained distinguished them from fireworks. Those that did explode could implode the walls of a house or tear apart a car. Under normal conditions they could not reach Tel Aviv or Jerusalem, but they were sufficient to terrorize border towns.

"You can go to the rocket factory," Ahmed had told me officiously in the Hotel Palestine. Recently out of school, he was unemployed, like practically everyone in the Gaza Strip. I paid him to take care of things for me. For security they blindfolded me so I wouldn't be able to say where I'd been. Perhaps, for a few extra dollars, they only wanted to enhance the uniqueness of the visit, or perhaps they really were concerned that if I knew every coordinate by heart I would pass them along. In any case, I was pretty nervous by the time they removed the blindfold from my eyes after a half-hour of driving. A grimy garage—this was the rocket factory, with a few lathes and with little Palestinian kids romping about inside. "Abu Qassam," I was told by way of introduction to the bomb manufacturer, the father of the Qassam rockets. He was a constantly-grinning, toothless old man. He offered me tea, and then proudly led me around, showing me the rockets, which went by various names.

Sderot was an hour and a half from Jerusalem. There was hardly any traffic by the time we arrived, but it was snowing. Aviad and his family lived in a big tower block on the outskirts of town. Though Aviad's family had a large house in the vicinity, Éva had insisted that they not live together with his parents, so Aviad had put in an application for a service flat, which was approved. They lived on the top floor. We now took the elevator, loaded up with things. Aviad pressed the buzzer and Éva opened the door. The two kids immediately ran out upon recognizing their father's voice.

"Hi Dani," said Éva in Hungarian, with a smile and a customary peck on each cheeks. "It's been a while."

"Yes, but you're still lovely," I said.

I wasn't lying. With her curly brown hair, snow-white skin, and red lips, Éva was among those Jewish girls men kill for. Giving birth had left no traces on her.

"You're a dear. Say hi to Dani, kids."

"How do you do," they said in unison before turning back to their father.

"Come on in, Dani," said Éva. "I'll show you your room. I'm so happy you were able to come."

I went in. Their small flat was cozily furnished, warm, and well lit. The guest room opened from the living room. An artificial, decorated Christmas tree stood in front of a large bookshelf.

"Put down your things, catch your breath, and then come out to join us for dinner," said Éva.

The guest room had a double bed and an adjacent closet with a bronze menorah on top. After unpacking my things I went back out to get the bulletproof vest and the helmet Aviad had brought for me, and took those into the room as well. I then realized that I hadn't brought any sort of gift for the children. That made me uneasy. I went out to the living room, where Éva and Aviad were speaking. She was sitting in his lap. It was apparent just how much these two people loved each other even after seven years of marriage.

"Sorry," I said when they noticed me.

"Oh, come now," Éva replied.

"I didn't bring a gift for the kids. Aviad only said today that I should come."

"Typical," said Éva, patting Aviad's head.

"No cause for panic," said Aviad. "I brought one."

"You managed to buy it?" asked Éva with gleaming eyes.

"Not quite. But the point is, I have it."

I didn't have a chance to ask what he was talking about, since the two boys now scampered into the room and kept asking their parents what they were getting for Christmas.

"You'll see after supper," replied Éva, getting up to set the table.

We ate in the kitchen. Potato casserole. Éva put a bottle of wine on the table, too. Canaan Red brand, bottled in Galilee. It occurred to me that this was, practically speaking, the same wine Jesus of Nazareth had drank.

Éva dished the food out onto the plates. Four-year-old András and six-year-old Jacob were squirming at the table, hardly able to wait.

"Let us pray," said Aviad, bowing his head. They prayed in Hebrew. When they finished, we began to eat. The kids could not contain themselves.

"Can we get it already?" asked Jacob. "We're not hungry."

"Give it to them before they go crazy," said Éva.

Aviad stood up, went into one of the rooms, and returned with a somewhat tattered box.

"Robodog!" the boys shouted from the table on seeing it.

"Don't break it within two minutes," said Aviad, pressing the box into Jacob's hands. The two boys stood up from the table and ran into the living room.

"And it's for both of you!" Aviad called after them.

Aviad and Éva exchanged a smile, and she kissed her husband full on the lips.

"You're a hero for having managed to get it."

"Well, it wasn't easy," replied Aviad, pouring wine for the three of us. The sounds of clinking and clanking and fighting could be heard from the living room.

"I'll go make order in there between them before they kill each other," said Éva, standing up and going into the other room. We could hear Robodog barking.

"You wouldn't believe the trouble I had to go through to get this piece of shit," said Aviad.

We toasted.

"For the toy?"

"Every kid in Israel is crazy about it."

"It does seem pretty exciting. Maybe I'll take one for my son."

"You won't, because you can't get one anywhere. I wanted one for the boys for Hanukkah. I'd been in every plaza, every shopping center from Jerusalem to Tel Aviv. It was nowhere in stock. The clerks kept saying they'd have it only in January."

"You bought it under the table?"

"Hell I did. Not even the black marketeers had them. Those that did, wanted a thousand bucks. A thousand bucks for this shit."

"Did you pay it?"

"I can't afford a thousand dollars for a toy on my salary. There's just no way. You should have seen the boys scowl on the last day of Hanukkah when they saw that there was no Robodog. Even Éva got into a fight with me. She was like, 'I moved here to Israel to be with you, and you can't even get this much done.'"

"Sounds like hell."

"You're not kidding."

"How did you finally get a hold of it?"

"Well, you won't believe it. It's a fucking miracle. You know, I'm in special forces at the moment."

"Do I want to know this?"

"Yeah, so keep quiet. Anyway, I'm a major with Shayetet 13. Four days ago intelligence notified us that Dzheba Demokratiya wants to infiltrate Israel through a tunnel."

"Those are the communists?" I asked.

"That's right," said Aviad, filling the glasses once again.

"So then, the order came quickly for us to destroy the tunnel and neutralize the threat. A team of six of us went, at night. I was the senior officer on the scene."

"You went into Gaza?"

"We did. We attacked at 3 a.m. Intel said the tunnel started under a farm. It had two entrances. We attacked from both sides. We totally surprised the jihadists. Two of the eight were awake. I broke down the door, shot in a stun grenade, and went in. I put four bullets into one of the guards, and when I saw the two dudes sleeping by the wall spring up, they got two each. In the head. It was like, 'Merry Christmas, motherfuckers.'"

"Serious business."

"We don't goof around. The others took care of the rest of them and secured the scene. I started looking for the tunnel entrance and anything Intel could use. Well, there was no fucking tunnel."

"What the fuck, they were civilians?"

"Hell they were. The Kalashnikovs were right there in a neat row leaning up against the wall. The guards had weapons, too. They would have used them sooner or later to shoot us."

"The whole region is full of weapons."

"Yep. So, imagine, while I'm rummaging through the house, there, looking at me, from beside the wall, in a pile of stuff next to one of the bastards with a hole in his head, is a brand new Robodog, in factory packaging. I snatched it up and brought it with me."

"Can you put a bomb in this piece of shit?"

"Hell no. It's a fucking toy. Just to be on the safe side, though, I had it looked at by the guys at the base, but they didn't find anything suspicious. Today I brought it with me along with your vest."

"Why the hell did a Palestinian militant have this toy on him?"

"Beats the hell out of me. In any case, I got to complete the holidays this way. The kids are happy, Éva is calm, all is beautiful. Merry Christmas."

"Merry Christmas," I said.

We clinked glasses. We drank the remaining wine. We agreed to put off our gossiping to the next day, since Éva was already putting the boys to bed. I went into my room and opened the window. I shivered as the wind struck me head on. I lit up a cigarette. I could see into the distance. The Israeli villages and towns glowed with yellow lights; the Gaza Strip lay dark in the falling snow. I looked at my watch. It was midnight. Some two thousand years ago, tradition had it, a certain Jewish woman had just been completing her labor.

My cell phone beeped. I closed the window and took it out of my pocket to see who'd written.

"The Hamas foreign affairs press office wishes all foreign correspondents a Merry Christmas and Happy Holidays."

The Peacock Angel

The night had finally begun to disperse over the hills. The air was getting palpably warmer, and yet the breaths of the men lying around the fire, under thick wool horse-blankets, were still visible. It was silent in the camp, the only sounds to be heard being the heavy breathing of the sleeping men.

The sun was rising. At first it illuminated the hills in the distance; then the road, lined with craters and burnt-out tanks; and, finally, the festering ruins of the captured village, beside which greasy black smoke rose up into the air. The mass grave was smoking still. Inside it were blackened villagers doused with diesel oil: the shrunken bodies of men, women, and children. The smell of burnt flesh was no longer in the air, since the wind had ceased.

Amanj stood up beside the M777 howitzer, which he'd been leaning up against until now. He stretched out and added wood to the fire, which crackled. The men coughed and stirred. It was dawn at Jalawla.

I felt a hand on my back.

"*Kak Sardar,*" said Amanj, giving me a gentle shake. "Wake up, Kak Sardar, it's morning."

I opened my eyes. The peshmerga were all waking up. Zirak, the Shiite, took the tea kettle, blackened from the fire, and filled it with water. He fished tea leaves out of the upper pocket of his tactical vest, sprinkled them in, and put the kettle on the fire. Hussein, the Sunni, went about cleaning his AK-74 with a greasy rag and a listless expression, while Hesin, the colonel, paced back and forth anxiously, a satellite phone in his hand. He was on the line with headquarters, in Khanaqin, trying to find out when the pickup truck would finally come to take away the dead. Many had died in the previous day's offensive. The corpses lay under blankets at the edge of the camp. The peshmerga took all their dead to Kurdish territory; they did not bury them in mass graves. This was exactly why Hesin was anxious for the pickup to arrive on time. It is not good if the dead remain long in the desert sun.

I sat up from the ground and wiped the sand off my face. I was dirty and unwashed, like anyone else from the unit. We'd been on the front for four nights.

"Drink this, Kak Sardar," said Zirak with a grin, pressing into my hand a plastic cup he then filled with tea.

As he reached out his hand, I could see on it the figure tattooed there along with the name of his one-time sweetheart, in Farsi. One night we drank beer together while watching the lights of the projectiles raining down, and he meanwhile told the story of how he'd had the tattoos made in Abu Ghraib, in prison, back during the regime of Saddam Hussein. "It was made with a safety pin dipped in boiled ink mixed with water and ash," he recounted. "It hurt like all hell." His sweetheart was of course someone else's wife by the time Zirak left prison.

I picked up the tea and sipped. It had a smoky taste but it warmed my belly. I took out a pack of cigarettes, offered one to the Shiite, and lit up.

"It's still giving off smoke," I said, pointing toward the village.

"Yeah. I figure they poured in all the diesel."

"Why?"

"So they'd all burn. People don't burn too well."

"Were they Arabs?"

"Fuck no," he said, and spat. "Ours."

He stood up, adjusted his American tactical vest, went over to the edge of the hill, and took a piss. I watched as the other peshmerga prepared the M777 for firing. Two of them pulled the military canvas off the howitzer's barrel while three more, on a truck a bit further back, began lifting off the projectiles and placing them side by side beside the weapon. I turned toward the sun, which was looming pale and feebly on the horizon. It was still cold, but I knew that within a couple of hours it would be hot as hell. My shirt would get soaked with sweat and dry against my skin repeatedly. The salt oozing out of me would draw patterns on it, like the veins on calcified seashells.

I'd arrived in Iraq a week earlier to photograph the Kurds' offensive. The country had been aflame for months. That caliphate declared from nothing, Islamic State, had shown mercy to nothing and no one in the course of its campaign. Its path was marked by mass graves; crucified men, women and children; villages burnt to the ground; and institutionalized slavery.

In contrast to the regularly collapsing Iraqi army, the Kurds were able to stop the Islamists' advance. True, for that the whole of Kurdistan had to enter the war. Grandfathers, grandmothers, women, and teenagers were firing on the front.

I knew I'd make good money with the photos. I got in contact with the Kurdistan Communist Party, and a couple of days later I was already on the front, embedded with a unit of fighting peshmerga. Islamic State took the beheading of Western journalists seriously: my head was worth 50,000 US dollars. I was assigned to accompany Colonel Hesin, so he could protect me. The colonel really took a liking to me when I asked him to shoot me dead without regrets if the situation was such. He shouldn't let me be taken alive. Not only he, but also the guys belonging to his team of bodyguards, were of the same mind in this matter. They gave me a Kurdish appellation, since they couldn't get my real, Hungarian name down right. They recognized that I'd joined up with them. They did not make me feel as if I were a mosquito having come for blood.

The unit was a ragtag bunch from all over Kurdistan. Amanj was a twenty-something Marxist from Erbil; Hussein was a deeply religious Sunni, likewise from Erbil; and Zirak was a Shiite, though he believed more in his rifle than in Allah. The colonel had been sent to the front from Sulaymaniyah; and Sardar, who belonged to the Kakei minority, was, at sixty-four, the oldest of them all. He was from Jalawla, the city the peshmerga were laying siege to just now. They, like all Kurds, were united by their common, searing hatred for Islamic State.

Every night, when the last attack came to a close, and they'd gathered up their dead, we often sat down together to drink smuggled liquor and look upon the lights of the burning city. With crass and vulgar jokes we shooed away death, which was prowling about us.

"Get ready, everyone," said Hesin, stepping to the fire and pouring himself some tea. "We are leaving in an hour."

I picked up the camera beside me and looked at its battery. According to the readout, it had a hundred pictures. Replacing the memory card, I put the previous day's photos in my satchel.

"Hey, take a look at that," said Amanj, nudging my shoulder and pointing toward the edge of the camp.

Standing right beside the truck that held the howitzer ammunition was old Sardar, bare-chested, facing the sun. He held his hands palm-upward, level with his waist. His lips were moving. His huge, thick mustache was twitching all about, we saw, but what he was saying, we couldn't hear.

"Look at that old devil-worshipper," said Zirak with a grin and sat down beside me on the ground.

"What is he doing?" I asked. Until then I hadn't seen the old man praying; he hadn't really seemed religious.

"Well, he is worshipping the devil, or the peacock," said Amanj, adding sardonically, "Or what do the Yazidis worship?"

"The peacock."

"Respect his religion," said Husein, looking up while cleaning his weapon and turning toward Amanj.

"He doesn't make snide remarks about the great Marx and Engels, either."

"Why, just look at this, the Daesh agent has spoken. Have you already written off clowning about in the morning?"

"Fuck you."

"Okay, but that old Kakei has gone completely bonkers all the same."

We watched as the old man repeatedly leaned down and kissed the ground. When he finished praying, he put on his green, military tunic, picked up his PKM from the ground, and headed our way. We all loved that old peshmerga, but everyone was surprised to see him praying.

"So, what is it, Sardar, did yesterday's liquor get to you?" asked Amanj.

"Or did you hit your head?" Zirak doubled down. "Maybe you've got sunstroke?"

"Oh, cut it out already," said Hussein, again looking up from his weapon.

"Good morning," said the old man, leaning down to the tea kettle and pouring himself a cup. He was in an unusually festive mood. "I'm happy I'll be passing this day with all of you."

"Well, not me," replied Zirak. "I'm sick of your ugly mugs. Being in my wife's bed, now that would be the best."

"You mean the bed of your brother's wife?" quipped Hussein with a grin.

"At least we don't have to take our women to nursery school afterward."

They laughed heartily. The old man gulped from his tea.

"Last night *Melek Taus* visited me in a dream, and he said I would die today in battle."

"I think it's Johnny Walker who paid you a visit," said Amanj with a grin.

"No. The Peacock Angel came, and said that today he would summon me to him."

"That's nonsense."

"I love you, Brother Amanj, and it's been an honor fighting by your side. There's no problem."

"You're not going to die, you old schmo. This is just senility setting in."

The old man smiled and lit a cigarette. Amanj sprang up from beside the fire and went to the jeep, and the others dropped the subject, too. Hussein finished cleaning his weapon, rolled up the blanket he was sitting on, and Zirak busied himself too, packing his things in his military rucksack.

"Are all of you ready?" asked Hesin. Everyone nodded.

"We received an order to join the peshmerga gathering at Hosseinia and take part in the assault this afternoon. Amanj,

Hussein, and the Hungarian will come with me in the jeep; Zirak and Sardar will come with the other vehicle."

Everyone stood up.

"Let's get going," said Hesin. "Let's go kill us a few Daesh." He flung on his Kalashnikov and headed toward the jeep.

Hosseinia was just forty kilometers from the artillery camp we'd spent the night at, and yet it took us two hours of driving to get there. Mines and impassable roads made travel difficult. Hussein drove, the colonel sat beside him up front, and the two of us, Amanj and I, sat in the back.

"Do you think the old man really had a dream about his God?" I asked.

"You don't believe in this nonsense, do you?"

"No. Of course not."

"Good, then. The old man is all worked up."

"Why?"

"Because around here it's all Yazidi villages."

Images of the recaptured villages came to mind—the razed houses, the corpses of animals. Daesh made sure that even if the peshmerga won, there wouldn't be anyone left to liberate. After each battle we saw only the dead, corpses flung into mass graves. I'd stopped keeping track of how many bodies I'd photographed in the days prior. Taking them had been a waste of time, since pictures of the dead can't be sold, and yet by reflex I photographed every single corpse I saw. The peshmerga suffered considerable losses, too. They had neither normal weapons nor bulletproof vests. They shot with cheap, Chinese rifles or else what remained from the US invasion.

"He's seen too many dead among his own people, which is why he thinks he, too, will die," explained Amanj. "His mind is playing tricks on him."

Hesin looked back from the front seat.

"Stop this talk now."

"No way."

"Cut the fucking shit. Sardar is a Kurdish peshmerga. We're all Kurds. And that's all that counts."

Hussein nodded from behind the wheel. His satisfied expression was more than evident in the rearview mirror.

The bombed-out houses were a reminder that some months earlier Hosseinia had been a village. Two weather-beaten T-74 tanks watched over the paved road that led from the guard post toward Jalawla. They could no longer move, but the peshmerga used their cannons and machine guns. Gathered behind them were the Toyota pickups that had transported the fighters for the assault. The guard post was on the hill opposite the village ruins. A large, military tarp had been stretched out on the hillside. The men were waiting under it.

We arrived at 1 p.m. Not a shadow was to be had; the air was trembling from the heat. After parking the jeeps, we went to the guard post. The peshmerga were sitting under the tarp, eating. The food was simple: beef soup and bread. Two women were ladling the soup out of two huge pots. They were dressed the same as the men. After introducing myself to each of the fifty or so peshmerga one by one, I sat down to await the briefing.

Amanj showed up with Zirak, both of them holding mess kits. Amanj handed me one of the two bowls he had with him and plopped down beside me. Hesin and Hussein sat on the other side of the tarp, talking with the others.

"Eat, Kak Sardar," said Amanj.

I ate. The soup was hot. It burned my mouth. We broke off bread from the same loaf.

"Where is the old man?" I asked.

"He's praying," said Zirak with a grin. "To placate his God."

"Won't he eat with us?"

"He's fasting," said Amanj with disgust, slurping up what was left of his soup. He wiped his face and lit a cigarette.

"Religion is the opiate of the masses," Amanj added. "This whole war is because of religion. Because of fucking God. Humanity is killing its own on account of made-up fathers and uncles, but if you believe in God, you don't need to have a conscience."

"So you don't believe in a thing," said Zirak.

"I believe in people. That eventually we'll get beyond class struggle and selfishness. According to Marx, that's inevitable."

"I don't believe in people. If God didn't exist, we'd make something up so we could kill in its name."

"Then what do you believe in?"

"In my rifle."

They choked with laughter. The last thing I wanted was to get caught up in discussing religion. I stood up and left the tarp.

Behind the tanks were adolescents and old folks with determined expressions, and I photographed them until a gunshot rang out by the tarp. This signaled the start of the briefing. It was on my way back to the tarp that I noticed old Sardar. He was sitting on top of the hill, staring at the sun, not bothered one bit by the scorching heat.

The briefing was held by a mustachioed, silver-haired colonel wearing a traditional Kurdish outfit. It wasn't overcomplicated. Because we were only sixty kilometers from the Iranian border, a US air attack was completely ruled out. Though all of us knew this, he repeated it for the officers all the same. The plan was simple. The jihadists had begun their retreat, and had entrenched themselves in Jalawla for house-to-house fighting. The general staff did not anticipate significant resistance. The peshmerga mission was to capture the checkpoints by the viaduct five kilometers outside of town, thus opening the road for heavy artillery. The colonel showed the location on Google Maps using his iPad. According to intelligence reports, the checkpoints were defended by about twenty men and two 50-caliber machine guns fixed into concrete barricades. The battle plan was that the fifty peshmerga would approach over the hills, and from the height nearest the bridge, they would take out those 50-caliber machine guns with rifles and RPGs. Then the four jeeps, equipped with air-defense batteries, would finish off the surviving jihadists and ensure the advance.

After the briefing the religious peshmerga gathered beside the tent to pray. They stood in a long line beside each other. They put their weapons behind themselves. I lit a cigarette and watched them for a while.

After smoking the cigarette, I headed back to the jeep to get my IV bulletproof vest. Amanj, who'd beaten me there and had already donned his black, Russian-made vest, was carrying over my equipment. I pulled the vest around me tight, securing its velcro fasteners, and then clipped on my helmet. In front of the tarp the peshmergas were double-checking their weapons. They then lined up on each side of the road, behind the hills.

Everything went smoothly at first. I'd been able to go along with the march for three kilometers when Hesin stepped over to me.

"You stay here with the colonel on that hill. From here you'll see everything."

He wasn't telling the truth. He knew that and so did I. I didn't have a telephoto lens.

"Don't you worry so much about me, Hesin."

"It's not you I'm worried about. You'd simply be a burden to the men. You're not fighting."

"I wouldn't be a burden."

"I've decided. If you want to get yourself killed, do so when your ass isn't sewn to my neck."

He smiled.

"Or not even then."

I nodded. Arguing was pointless. I stepped over beside the colonel, who nodded and pointed out the hill we had to climb. We left the procession and headed upward. Even through my shoes I could feel the searing heat of the sand.

It really was possible to see everything well from the top of the hill, only that we were too far away to take pictures. I saw clearly the viaduct's arches, the 50-caliber machine guns in the middle of the road, and even the black, Islamic State flags on the barricades. I cursed myself for not having brought along a telephoto lens. There was no choice now other than to set my camera at its highest resolution. The colonel and his two assistants, lying on their bellies, positioned themselves comfortably atop the hill, took out their military binoculars, and extended the antennae of their satellite phones. We waited.

The assault began with shouts of "*Allahu Akbar*" erupting from several throats. Then came the crackling of the machine guns, the sizzling of the RPGs, and the blasts as the grenades hit their targets. Smoke rose from above the machine-gun nests, and I could see barely a couple of enemy muzzle flashes. I heard the colonel, beside me, talk into his phone and give commands. A couple of minutes later, the machine-gun-equipped Toyota pickups sped by us on the road below, the gunners in the back having begun shooting at the viaduct even as the trucks raced along.

Characteristically, it all went to shit when things were just about wrapped up. Two armored Humvees seized from the Iraqi Army emerged from under the viaduct's pillars, equipped with 50-caliber cannons. In the space of a moment they shot out the Toyotas and forced the men back behind the hills. The sky filled with the greasy smoke of the burning vehicles. Such a Humvee, I knew, could withstand even two RPGs by the time it gave up, providing it was hit to begin with.

The dead were brought back from the front on a pickup. It made four trips back and forth, its bed becoming slick with blood. Those among the injured who were unable to walk were brought back on the same vehicle. The peshmerga lost fourteen men, and the number of injured exceeded twenty. That was the cost of taking the viaduct.

I waited outside by the tarp for the guys to return. Inside, the two women who'd ladled out the soup were now preparing to tend to the injured. The were gathering up medications, anti-coagulants, American battlefield first-aid kits.

Amanj arrived looking at once sooty and pale while supporting Zirak, who'd been shot in the hand. As frail as Amanj seemed, after one of the women peeled off his tunic, it was apparent that the bullet which had passed through him had gone through the shoulder, only breaking the bone. Hesin and Hussein had pulled through uninjured, while old Sardar had received a nasty shot in the chest. Ashen-gray, he just stared blankly ahead as four men carried him off the truck and lay him down under the tarp.

"We can't help this one," shouted one of the women. "He's got to get blood and be operated on!"

"How much time does he have?" asked Hesin.

"An hour," said the woman. "We've clamped the artery, but he needs surgery immediately."

"We're leaving," said Hesin, and headed down the hill. Amanj helped Zirak up off the ground and they followed Hesin.

Hussein and I set the old man onto a camp stretcher. The Yazidi was a large, strapping man, well over 200 pounds. His tunic was blood-soaked, which left my hand bloody.

"Don't leave his rifle here," said Hussein before we lifted the stretcher. I leaned down, picked up the PKM machine gun with its sawed-off barrel, and, holding it by its sling, flung it over my shoulder.

By the time we reached the bottom of the hill, Hesin had agreed with one of the peshmerga that we would take his pickup, that the peshmerga would come along in Hesin's vehicle, and that in Khanaqin they would switch back. Carefully we lifted the old man's body onto the bed of the truck. Hesin drove, with three of us sitting inside: Zirak, Hussein, and I. Amanj sat by Sardar in the back.

The vehicle's tires kicked up dust: Hesin didn't want to lose even a minute. Zigzagging as he sped along, he kept honking to clear the traffic in front of us out of the way.

We were silent. No one was in the mood to say a thing.

The first checkpoints appeared when we left the war zone. We went by a guard shack without even slowing down, but ten minutes later a more serious one loomed up ahead, with concrete antitank barriers and a crossing gate. The checkpoint was manned by Shiite soldiers from the Iraqi Army. Hesin was fuming at having to slow down.

"Good day," began the Iraqi soldier in Arabic. "We have to check the car for bombs."

"Well, can't you see, you moron, that we're taking injured from the front and are in a hurry?"

"I'm sorry, but rules are rules."

"If I have to stop here now, we'll shoot you all to shreds," said Hesin. Everyone knew he wasn't kidding. Hussein raised his Kalashnikov at once and aimed it at the Iraqi soldier.

"No need to get so nervous," said the Iraqi, grinning, and waving for the crossing gate to be lifted. Hussein lowered his weapon, and Hesin pressed the pedal. The sand dunes now gave way to scant vegetation, the huts to small towns. We raced along unabated. A half-hour after leaving the checkpoint, Amanj beat a hand against the car and shouted that we needn't go so fast, because the old man had died.

It was dark by the time we arrived in Khanaqin. Peshmerga military headquarters was in a hillside villa on the city outskirts. After passing through the checkpoint that guarded the road leading to the hill, we parked by other cars. Medics came from the hospital, lifted off the dead Yazidi, and helped lead Zirak away.

Hesin and I went into headquarters to meet with the general staff. The Kurd leaders were getting ready for supper. Since I was a foreigner and, what is more, had returned from the front, they invited me to join them, too. They served exceptional Kurdish specialties, because the commander of the chiefs of staff had brought along his chef from Sulaymaniyah. But I had barely any appetite. When supper was over, I excused myself and, citing exhaustion, went out to the villa's yard. On the way out, I lifted a bottle of J&B Scotch whiskey from among the many bottles of various sorts out on the bar. No one noticed.

The villa had a large yard, with a colossal lawn where the army tents were pitched. Peshmerga were sitting around campfires. Shreds of patriotic Kurdish songs and the din of conversation filled the night.

I found Amanj in the parking lot, under the cedars. He was sitting on the hood of a jeep, smoking. Hussein was asleep in the back seat.

"So, what's up?" I asked, and showed the bottle in my hand.

"Kak Sardar, you always know what I'm thinking," said Amanj with a grin, taking the bottle from my hand, unscrewing the cap, taking a mighty swig, and giving it back. I drank, and then sat down beside him.

"It's been a long day," I said, taking out a cigarette and putting it in my mouth. Amanj lit it.

"That's for sure," he said.

The bottle passed between us, and finally Amanj broke the silence, after we'd downed half the whiskey. He took a big gulp, wiped his mouth, and said, "At least it turned out that there is a God."

The Kingdom of God Is Approaching

The front ran along the Euphrates. The river here widened into a marsh. It rolled on, green, in the midday sun. Reeds grew lushly on the eastern bank, and thick shrubs lined the road. Waterfowl nested there, and tadpoles flailed about with their tiny fins in the shallow water so as to fend off the current. If you stared for long at the water, you could see the glinting bellies of fish as they bobbed up out of the mud to hunt.

The smell of boiled lentils was in the air. Two soldiers with the garrison were making soup. The men were excitedly leaning over the blackened cauldron, stirring and tasting. The September sun drew spots on their green coveralls.

Women were sitting about under a tarp on the roof of the unplastered concrete shack that served as the artillery battery's main headquarters. There were four of them, and they too were wearing green coveralls. They were laughing while weaving each other's long, black hair into buns. Only the oldest, an already graying woman, was keeping lookout, panning the western side of the marsh with binoculars.

"It's almost ready, comrade," one of the men shouted up to the roof. The older woman, who was called Nesrin and who was the battery's commander, lowered the binoculars and leaned out from under the tarp.

"I hope you don't make it too salty this time, Rauf."

It was a warm September day. You got to feeling there wasn't even a war. But there was a war. It was smoke that reminded us of this, greasy black smoke rising up toward the sky. The city on the western side of the marsh was burning. The column of smoke could be seen from even fifteen kilometers away. Jarabulus was burning, but so were the villages around it. Islamic State was on the retreat. It wanted to leave nothing behind for the Kurds.

"Lunch is ready!" Rauf yelled and began beating the side of the cauldron with the spoon. Young, armed women came forward from the thicket, where three M-55 howitzers stood. They set their machine guns up against the side of the building and sat on the ground. The soldiers climbed down from the roof, too, leaving just one person up there, with the binoculars, to stand guard.

The two men ladled the soup into mess-tins, pressed them into the soldiers' hands with a portion of bread for each of them, and then they, too, began to eat.

"You're not hungry, comrade?" asked Nesrin.

She stopped above me. Her narrow face was grooved with wrinkles; her mouth was thin. Her thick black hair was graying vigorously. All this imparted a sternness to her lineaments, balanced only by her cheerily glistening brown eyes.

"I ate a whole lot in Kobani."

"You could at least taste our concoction. True, Comrade Rauf is a far better marksman than a cook, but he does do it."

She pressed her mess-tin in my hand, got more for herself, and sat down beside me. We began to eat.

"Isn't it too salty?"

"No, it's just right."

"Hear that, Rauf?" asked Nesrin, adding, with a laugh, "The Hungarian comrade likes your soup. On that note, so do I."

"I try, comrade," Rauf replied with satisfaction.

For a while we ate in silence.

"I'd like to photograph you, Nesrin," I said, when I finished the soup.

"Not a chance."

"But in Qamishli they said …"

"My nose is too big in pictures."

"I'll photograph you in profile."

"Why do you want to photograph an old woman? There are the nice young comrades here."

"I like your face."

"I've got a husband. Besides, you could be my son."

She laughed.

"Don't take me seriously, I'm just kidding with you. You can photograph me. As long as you promise that my nose won't be big in the picture."

"I promise."

Sounds of static filtered out of the radio on the commander's belt.

"*Assalamu alaikum wa rahmatulla*, brothers, whereabouts are you?" crackled a male voice.

Nesrin unsnapped the radio from her belt, put it on the ground in front of her, and turned up the volume.

"This is Daesh," she said. "They're so close that we pick up their radio transmissions."

"Really?" I asked, but I didn't get a reply, because the radio came again.

"*Va alaikum salam,* brother," replied another male voice. "We'll arrive in the village soon."

"Are you nervous, Brother Abed?" the radio continued.

"The idiots' transmission button got stuck," said Nesrin.

Everyone turned toward the radio.

"*Bismillah*, I am really a bit nervous, Brother Islem," a younger voice replied. "I'm happy you give me direction."

"I'm always happy to help younger brothers."

"May Allah bless you for it. You are a true mujahid, whom everyone looks up to. Since when have you been in the caliphate?"

"*Alhamdulillah*, two years already. Though I've prayed for Him to call me to Him, until now Allah has kept me here. How long have you been with us, brother?"

"By the mercy of Allah, four months. I too would like to be a martyr, if Allah allows it."

"*Mashallah*. How do you like life in the caliphate?"

"Amazing. Finally I can be among true brothers."

"Where are you from?"

"Egypt."

"*Mashallah*. Mother of the world. Say, have you found yourself a wife yet?"

"Unfortunately, not yet. The Muslims all have husbands already. True, I haven't had time, either, to look around much."

"You could marry a martyr's widow."

"Yes."

"Or you could buy yourself a lovely young slave."

"I don't have that much money, brother."

"Have you been with a woman at all yet?"

"No, brother, not yet. I'm nervous, too."

"Oh, come now, don't be nervous. Anyone is capable of sticking the stick into the ditch. And if you're that afraid, there's Viagra. You'll see, the brothers will stuff your pockets full on your wedding."

"Yes. Do you have a wife, brother?"

"Not yet. But soon. There's no rush. I have two Yazidi slaves who amuse me."

"They amuse you."

"They do. For the Prophet, peace and blessings upon him, said we can bed our servants as much as we so wish."

I passed my eyes over the Kurdish women soldiers. Everyone's face clouded over. Even Commander Nesrin's eyes had stopped glistening. No one said a word.

"*Mashallah*. And are you not afraid that they will turn against you in your sleep?"

"Not I. I keep strict discipline among the slaves."

"You never had any problem with them? I heard of a case in which they conspired at night and cut the mujahid's throat."

"Yes. At first I had three. One of them escaped, but we caught up with her at the city borders. Since then I've had just two."

"*Mashallah*."

"You know what I'm saying? If it also be Allah's will, and we get back to Raqqa, I'll sell you one of them. The younger one. She's hardly a woman yet. With that you'll win enough time so you can choose wisely among the Muslims."

"You are really generous. May Allah bless you. But I can't pay for it. I'm poor."

"You'll cover it in installments, from your pay. The last thing the caliphate will reduce is our pay, because we are the foundations of the caliphate."

"Indeed, so we are. In the name of Allah."

The radio suddenly reverted to static. Everyone at the garrison was silent. Nesrin stood, and called up to the roof.

"Is there any movement?"

"A Toyota is coming from the northeast," came the reply.

"Are they within firing range?"

"No, comrade, but another five or ten minutes if they don't stop."

"Let me know right away when they're within firing range."

"Yes, ma'am."

The soldiers returned to the howitzers. Nesrin picked up the radio from the ground. The garrison was filled with its static. She walked back and forth with it until the signal returned.

"It is written that the unbelievers will attack the armies of Mehdi and the caliphate with full force, but that Allah will then blow upon them and they will collapse. So don't worry. Trust in Allah."

"*Amin.* And yet we've retreated quite a lot lately."

"We'll retreat, and we'll advance again. No one thought we could take Mosul. We did so without firing a shot. We have brothers in Libya, Egypt, and Chechnya. Allah is with us, and Islamic State shall rule the earth."

"*Amin.*"

"Are you ready? We'll be there soon."

"Can't we stop to pray? I'm a little nervous."

"Why?"

"Because this is the hardest part for me."

"These are infidels, the enemies of the caliphate."

"I know. But they still don't have weapons. I can't stand their wailing."

"I don't like killing them, either, but it must be so. For Allah."

"Can't they just be chased away?"

"No. In the Kingdom of God there is no room for infidels. Remind yourself that we are doing this for Kingdom of God. The Kingdom of God is approaching, and each day it is closer, if we perform our duty well."

"*Amin.*"

Commander Nesrin sprang up from the ground. She climbed to the top of the shack. We heard the crackle of machine guns—AK-47s—erupting in the distance. The water brought us the sound. From the top of the shack, Commander Nesrin issued commands to the howitzer teams, who had taken aim. In the end, though, she did not give the order to shoot, because they were beyond firing range and she didn't want to waste the ammunition.

After five minutes on standby the soldiers returned, and sat down in front of the shack. No one said a word. Everyone could hear the shots from afar.

The whole thing lasted a half-hour. Finally all that could be heard was, once again, the rustling of the reeds and the croaking of the frogs. The wind picked up in the afternoon. It brought with it a heavy, burnt smell.

The Trial

We put the two machine guns on the kitchen table. "I'll take them to headquarters," said the colonel to the boys, who then stepped back outside as he closed the door. The engine started up and the jeep took off, carrying the fellows we'd spent four nights with in the desert.

It was a radiant Thursday afternoon. The sun was shining over Sulaymaniyah, and we'd returned safe and sound from the front at Khanaqin. Not even the truck had a scratch.

The colonel—Hesin was his name—lived in a two-story, American-style single family home. He'd furnished it with good taste and modern accoutrements. Compared to those unwashed desert nights and the smoky tea we'd warmed in tin cans over open fires, we were now beset by unimaginable luxury. Since arriving in Iraqi Kurdistan, I'd spent nearly every waking moment with the colonel. He spoke English well, so I, the foreign correspondent, had been assigned to him. We went together to the front, where, all night in the desert, together we awaited the attack. We ate the same food and drank the same drinks. Because the peshmerga fighting on the front couldn't pronounce my Hungarian name, he accorded me the princely title *Sardar,* adding the honorific term *Kak* before it, hence making me *Kak Sardar*. But after the first battle he also called me "Brother," as he did the peshmerga. We liked each other.

"I feel really sick, brother," said the colonel with a grin as I removed the camera from my backpack and set the battery and memory card on the table.

"You look horrible," I replied.

"You seem sick, too."

"Yes, I am."

"You need medicine."

"Yes, urgently."

The colonel stepped to the refrigerator, opened the door, and pulled out a bottle of Jack Daniels.

He poured a decent amount into two glasses, adding ice in each, and then handed one glass to me.

"Fuck ISIS!"

We drank. The whiskey washed the past four days' constant drizzle of sand down our throats. The moment I put down my glass and he did his, the colonel refilled each one.

"Fuck Abu Bakr al-Baghdadi!"

"Fuck Abu Bakr al-Baghdadi!"

Again we drank.

"Forgive me for saying so, Kak Sardar," said the colonel with a grin as he again put down his glass, "but you stink."

"I know. I'm off to wash up."

"Very well, I'll order something to eat in the meantime."

"You stink, too."

I gave the colonel a slap on the back and headed upstairs. On the way up the marble steps it seemed inconceivable to me that a war was going on 200 kilometers away.

And yet there was a war. Two weeks earlier the Islamic State offensive had been halted barely twenty kilometers from Erbil. All of Kurdistan had been focused on the war: men young and old, women and children, had all gone to the front. They had to. Everyone knew what to expect of the caliph, Abu Bakr al-Baghdadi. We'd seen it full well for ourselves.

The charred corpses of Sunni Muslims had been piled up by the bushel in ditches dug by backhoes: those the caliph had no use for had been doused with gasoline and set alight. Worst of all was the sight of burnt children. It was easy to tell their bodies apart from those of the women and elderly on account of their smaller size. The fire had shrunk them even more.

The bathroom was spacious, with white tile walls and a metal shower stall. As I loosened my laces and then slipped off my boots, the sand poured out. I undid my belt and unbuttoned my shirt. I really did stink.

For three days and nights I'd been in the desert in the same clothes, my shirt drenched with sweat and then drying and then getting soaked yet again. As I now saw, the salt had formed white splotches on my chest and underarms.

I finished undressing and turned the tap. The hot water fogged up the shower's glass door at once. The sand still clinging to my skin began flowing off, and it seemed as if the water was washing away even the images etched into my brain, from mass graves to the expressions on the faces of dead peshmerga. Pressing my forehead to the tile wall, I stood under the shower for a long time.

I was drying myself with one of the colonel's towels when he stopped by the bathroom door, which was slightly ajar, holding two glasses of whisky.

"Drink this, then come down. We've got to have a word about something."

He pressed the glass into my hand, we clinked glasses, and drank up. He then hurried back down the stairs. After getting dressed, I went down as well.

He was in the living room staring at his laptop, which he shut on seeing me.

"I've got to go to headquarters."

"What happened?"

"The boys caught one of them."

I sat down at the table and refilled both glasses with whiskey, handing one to the colonel.

"Can I go with you?"

"You can't write anything about it. This is top secret. Journalists can't go in there."

"I understand."

"I'll say you're a volunteer under my command."

We clinked glasses.

"Get ready. We're going in a moment. Have something to eat."

I got up and went to the kitchen. I opened the fridge. I found a chunk of cheese. I sat down and ate. The bell rang. The colonel opened the door.

He spoke in Kurdish with whoever it was. He then came into the kitchen.

"We're going, brother."

I got up from the table. At the door was a soldier who looked about thirty and was in a traditional peshmerga outfit. I threw on my blazer and headed off.

We went in a Toyota flatbed pickup. All three of us sat up front, the soldier at the wheel and the colonel between us. The two of them spoke, in Kurdish, for the length of the thirty-minute drive, which took us between the mountains through the twilight city. I stared at stores' neon lights and at all the people milling about and chatting in front of cafés. It didn't seem like war.

Finally we turned onto the mountain road leading to the military headquarters, which soon came into view, surrounded by a six-foot-high fence topped off with barbed wire. In the watchtowers, guards holding Russian-made PKM machine guns stared out over the landscape, their breaths visible against the glare of the spotlights.

A cluster of tanks surrounded the entrance booth. The guard stepped to the window, Kalashnikov in hand, as we stopped. Pointing at me, the colonel said something in Kurdish. The guard gave me a once-over and waved us on.

We stopped by the front door. The colonel got out and went inside. I followed him down a dimly lit hallway and then down a long flight of stairs to the cellar, where the holding cells were.

"We caught him in Jalawla," said the colonel. "He wanted to sneak in to our base in Khanaqin."

"I see."

"He was armed. We suspect he wanted to assassinate someone. So far he hasn't confessed a thing."

Beside the stairs was a desk, by which sat another soldier. He saluted on seeing the colonel, who waved a hand, leaned over the desk and signed a sheet of paper. He motioned for me to follow him.

"The reason you can follow me is that at the moment I'm the highest-ranking officer in the city. The entire high command is at Khanaqin."

The soldier led us down the hallway, which was flanked by rusted metal doors. He then stopped by one, took out a key, and opened it.

It was dark inside. Only after several long seconds could we make out the furnishings. In the middle of the room was a big long table, beside it a metal chair, to which a boy of about seventeen was handcuffed. He blinked in the sudden light, and I could now clearly see his face, caked with dried blood.

The colonel stepped in. I followed. The soldier shut the door. The colonel turned on the room's only light, a single bulb.

"*As-salamu alaykum,*" said the colonel in Arabic by way of greeting. "How are you, follower of the caliph?"

"I really need to use the toilet," the boy replied. "Please let me go."

"What's your name, boy?"

"Ahmed Al Bahiza."

"Where are you from?"

"Bahiza"

"What were you up to in Khanaqin, Ahmed?"

"I've really got to go, please let me out."

"You went to Khanaqin to kill someone. Who?"

"No, my mother lives in Khanaqin. I was going to visit her."

"With a gun?"

"There's a war on."

"You won't be going to the toilet anytime soon, Ahmed."

"I beg you to let me out," said the boy hysterically. "I'm going to piss my pants."

"Take a load of this scum, this Arab killer, Kak Sardar," said the colonel, turning to me.

"I'm not a killer," said the boy.

The colonel slapped the boy, who toppled over along with his chair.

"Talk when I ask you to," said the colonel.

The child sobbed on the floor. He pissed his pants.

"How disgusting!" said the colonel. "Is this proper behavior on jihad?"

"I'm *not* on jihad," said the boy. The colonel leaned toward the boy and, taking care not to touch his urine-soaked trousers, pulled him back up, chair and all.

"When did you join ISIS?"

"I don't belong to ISIS."

"You're lying."

The colonel hit him again, but this time made sure he didn't topple over. The blood again started running from the boy's nose. The boy began to sob. He raised his head and looked at me.

"Please help me! I'm innocent!" he said in perfect English. The colonel hit him again, and the chair fell over. Grimacing, he repeated, "Please help me!"

"Where did you learn English, you dirty Arab?" asked the colonel, kicking him in the mouth, his teeth crackling loudly. The boy fell and lost consciousness.

"You shouldn't do this," I said as the colonel set the chair upright yet again. He went to the back corner of the room, where a faucet was hanging from the wall. Beside it was a grimy plastic bucket. The colonel turned the faucet and let water into the bucket.

"And why not?"

"The Geneva Convention."

"Fuck the Geneva Convention. This here isn't a soldier."

"Then he's a civilian."

"He's a dirty ISIS beast. You yourself have seen the mass graves and what they've done otherwise."

"But you can't know for sure that he's one of them."

"I know. This is a dirty Arab."

"Not every Arab is with ISIS."

"Tell that to those who've been beheaded or burned alive."

"Please stop it. The kid has the right to a trial."

"You idiotic Westerners. You come here to dole out your wisdom and rob our oil. *This* is the trial."

"Don't be a brute."

"I'm not a brute," he said, pointing at the boy. "*This* is."

The colonel took the bucket of water and poured it on the boy's head. The kid came to, blood pouring from his mouth.

"Who was the target?" he asked.

"There was no target. I'm not with ISIS. I learned English in the American School. I was on my way to Khanaqin to visit my mother," he said, choking on his own blood. Looking at me, he said, "Please, sir, don't let him do this to me."

"I'll tell you what," said the colonel, taking the Makarov pistol from his belt and loading the barrel. It was a beautiful pistol I'd done lots of target shooting with on the front with the boys.

"I'll count to three," said the colonel, pressing the pistol to the kid's temple. "I'll count to three, and if you don't tell me who or what the target was, I'll blow your head apart."

"Dear God!"

"*One.*"

"There *was* no target. I came to visit my mother!"

"*Two.*"

"I swear that there is one God and Mohamed is his prophet and that I'm not with ISIS."

"*Three.*"

My right hook struck the colonel on the chin. It caught him off guard, sending him flying right across the room. He landed on his back on the floor. The pistol fell from his hand. I jumped on him at once. He was ready. With one swing of his leg he kicked me off him. I fell back, toppling over the kid, chair and all. By the time I got up, the pistol was in his hand.

"I really do like you, Hungarian, but if you hit me one more time I'll shoot you."

I got up from the floor. The only sound in the room was that of the kid sobbing.

"I won't let you do this."

"You humanists. It's because of you that the whole world is where it is." He held the pistol toward the boy and fired three times. Two bullets ripped open his chest and one hit his head. My ears began to ring from the shots.

"You're a cold-blooded murderer."

"There's a war on."

The door opened and the guard ran in, machine gun in hand. The colonel said something to him in Kurdish. The guard saluted and left.

"Coming?" asked the colonel, locking his pistol and putting it back on his belt before stepping out the door. I followed. We went up the stairs. The car was already waiting by the front door. We didn't say a word to each other the whole way. The colonel spoke only with the driver. On getting back to the house, the colonel opened the door and went to the living room; I went upstairs, to the guest room.

I had one more day in Sulaymaniyah, from where I had to go to Erbil to catch a flight to Europe.

I undressed and got into bed. The image of that teenage boy didn't let me sleep. What could I do to feel better? I considered my options. There were none. The Kurdish military command and human rights organizations were too busy with the war to look into the case of a single murdered Arab. My throat was dry from the realization.

I looked at my watch: 2:30 a.m. Getting out of bed, I headed downstairs, intending to go to the kitchen, where the colonel kept a jug of drinking water. Even from the bottom of the stairs I could hear him snoring. I looked into the living room, where he was sleeping. He was gripping an empty bottle of whiskey in his sleep. On a little table by the couch was his laptop, which kept playing a video from some Arabic file server.

I stepped closer to see what it was.

It was an ISIS video—featuring the murdered teenager, holding the decapitated head of a Yazidi woman by the hair, displaying it to the camera. He was smiling.

I went to the kitchen for a glass of water.

Son of a Dog

Two dead mongrels swung in the wind. They had been hanged by the neck with wire cord at the entrance to the alleyway. These were fresh kills: the blood dripping out of their coats left spots in the mud. Men shouted loudly and anxiously; cars and motorbikes revved in the distance. It was Thursday night in the City of the Dead. The sun had set hours earlier behind the red crags of the Mokattam Hills.

These were months of madness. I could not sleep. By day I wandered the city like the living dead, and the nights too didn't bring relief.

The first person who gave me opium was called Khalid Ramzi. We'd met in a grimy inner-city café a month earlier. He asked for 150 Egyptian pounds, or geneihs, for the raw opium, which, wrapped in wax paper, he pressed into my hand. He gave me his mobile number.

With the opium I could treat my chronic insomnia. I had no idea what it was like to sleep normally any more, so those opium-infused days were exhilarating. I was able to work, able to sleep. There wasn't a happier man in the world. Then the opium ran out. The insomnia returned. The visions returned. After the third day I pulled out my mobile and called Khalid.

He told me to go to the City of the Dead. "I won't be far from the Sayeda Aisha Mosque, near the Bahtak. Go there by nine."

The City of the Dead is a necropolis where everything is muddy and gray. The paved access road does not lead in among the tumbledown tombs, but ends by the live-animal market.

The wealthy buried themselves here a long time ago. They built up imposing crypts. A city unto itself, which they had guarded by the area's poor. The poor then brought their families up to Cairo, and slowly but surely they moved in among the crypts. Thus it was that the cemetery filled with life.

Right at nine I got out of the taxi at the Sayeda Aisha Mosque. An old man was sitting out front, leaning against a stick, and I asked him where I could find the Bahtak, at which he pointed toward one of the alleyways. Mud squelched under my shoes. My nose filled with the stench of garbage and urine. After wandering for half an hour, I realized the Bahtak was not where the old man had indicated. I walked round and round, darted among the narrow alleyways formed by the sinking crypts. I called Khalid's mobile, but he didn't answer. That was when I noticed two dog carcasses swaying against the wall and heard men shouting. Beside the corpses, a thin little road ran all the way to the foot of the Mokattam Hills. I went that way. The road led to a square where garbage was burning—which, together with a barrel of burning oil, provided all the light illuminating a throng of men who had gathered in the middle of the square. A rat-faced man in a djellaba blocked my way.

"Well now, what are you doing here, khoaga?" he asked, using the local term for a rich foreigner. He sliced the air with the spear he was holding.

"I'm looking for Khalid Ramzi."

"What's your business?"

"I came to do some shopping."

The Arab looked over my sweat-splotched shirt and bloodshot, insomniac eyes, whereupon he nodded and made way.

The men were gathered around a ring formed by rusty metal barrels. They were shouting and shaking their fists. I went closer to see what was happening. Everyone was focused on two young teenage boys—barefoot, half-naked—pummeling each other in the ring. They were filthy and sweaty, with mud bubbling up from between their toes. One was a head taller than the other; he must have been the older boy, but he didn't look a day past fourteen. The two were hitting with their fists, full force. Neither put up a defense; each simply jumped up close to the other and then parted for the length of a punch. They circled each other. They were fighting for stakes. Their lips and eyebrows were torn, and the blood had soaked through dirty gauze bandages wrapped around their hands. I quickly understood there were neither rules nor breaks. No trainer or assistant stood in the corners to throw in the towel if all hell broke loose. The crowd was waiting for one child to knock the other out.

The taller one had the upper hand. He was also heavier, and with his long arms he was able to ward off the shorter one so he couldn't get a big punch in. How long they'd been at it, I didn't know, but both were gasping for breath. After one more exchange of punches they clung to each other and flopped down in the mud. That's when an onlooker stepped into the ring. With a reed cane half a meter long he went about hitting the two children until they got up. Tottering, they stood by the light of the fire, facing each other, their faces filthy with mud and blood. The smaller one lost his balance and crumpled to his knees. The crowd whistled as the other spread his arms in triumph and grinned.

"Finish it! Finish it!" the men shouted in unison.

The tall boy walked over to the one kneeling, stepped on his right leg, and with all his might struck him on the face. The dull thud could be heard even through the ruckus.

"Mustafa! Mustafa!" came the crowd's rapturous cry.

The taller boy turned, held his hands high, and jumped around the ring.

What happened next, no one expected. The knocked-out boy appeared behind Mustafa as if from nowhere. Only the blood running from his nose indicated what a big blow he'd just received.

"Hey, you!" he shouted.

Mustafa turned, and that was when the blow struck him. A perfect right hook—you could hear the crack of Mustafa's jawbone. The blow knocked him sideways, and he hit one of the oil barrels headfirst, losing consciousness immediately.

For a few seconds the crowd stood dumbfounded. Finally a clamor began: "Little lion! Little lion! Little lion!"

The short boy didn't strut around. In an instant he climbed over the barrels behind him and vanished. Groups quickly formed around a few men: those who'd placed bets were demanding their due.

Still seeing no sign of Khalid Ramzi, I stayed by the ring. The boy who'd fainted slowly came to, at first getting up on one knee and then, holding a barrel, onto his feet. His head was hideously smashed; one of his eyes looked like an open wound. For a few seconds he wavered uncertainly before he, too, climbed out of the ring, and headed toward a bulky man in a tank top. The man must have weighed 120 kilos. He had a thick wad of cash in his hands and was using it to pay various others. Mustafa said something. Turning with disgust, the man gave him a slap. The boy fell facedown on the ground. The man added a few kicks before a couple of others tugged him away.

Finally I noticed Khalid Ramzi standing opposite the ring, beside the burning heap of trash. He was in a brown djellaba and black slippers. His belly stuck out from beneath the outfit and his face was smoky with filth. Beside him stood the boy who'd won the previous match, drinking water from a grimy plastic bottle.

"Abu khoaga," Ramzi said on seeing me. "I was beginning to think you wouldn't come."

"You didn't answer your phone."

"Yes, there was a match. We won."

"I saw. Do you have opium?"

"That's what I wanted to talk to you about. The bloody Bedouins are bringing it only next week. And I need an advance, too."

"You can't do that to me."

"I'm sorry about it. What I have, I need too."

"You can't fucking do this to me. I can't sleep without opium."

The next few days passed through my mind at once. How I'd be lying on my back in my roach-infested hotel room, unable to sleep. Recurring in my visions: the end of a bourgeois life and the figures of a temptress and a little kid. That inexplicable, gripping, throbbing sensation in my head that didn't let me rest, that tightened its grip every day until I thought of suicide. Like staring into the abyss of hell, that's how I saw the stretch of insomnia before me.

Finally Ramzi took pity. "How much money do you have?"

"Two thousand pounds."

"Where do you live?"

"In a hotel. Downtown."

"Have you paid for it yet?"

"Yes, to the end of the month."

"Too bad."

"Why?"

"You could have stayed here until the Bedouins arrive. And gotten some of mine."

"I'll stay here."

"Let's have the money."

I took the money from my pocket and counted it into his hand. I didn't care. I just wanted to sleep; that's all that mattered. It didn't matter where, or in whose company. I wanted to lose consciousness.

Three of us plodded along through the mud, avoiding trash heaps and toppled crypts: Ramzi, the victorious boy, and me. Along the way we stopped at a food stand, where Ramzi gave the kid five pounds to buy kusherie.

"Eat, Amr, you deserve it," he said, caressing the boy's head.

"Thank you, sir."

Though clearly ready to drop from exhaustion and hunger, the boy didn't stuff himself with the lentils and rice. He took it with him in a plastic bag while stumbling along the road.

Khalid Ramzi's house was at the other end of the City of the Dead, where the flea market ended. This too was a crypt, with the name of the family that had owned it written on the entrance. Electricity ran in from the street by way of black wires that passed through the windows.

After rummaging in the pocket of his djellaba for a while, Ramzi produced a huge key and inserted it into the black iron gate. His crypt comprised two rooms, if, that is, the interior spaces where granite tombstones stood could be called rooms. The larger one was Ramzi's. In it was an arabesque sofa, and a dirty rug he'd draped over a tombstone. The tombstone—engraved with the name of an influential nobleman of the early nineteenth century—was the TV stand.

"Sir," Amr said. "if you don't have any other work for me tonight, I'd go to bed."

"Sure thing, go ahead," Ramzi replied.

"Good night, sirs."

He left the room, heading for the smaller space, where a pair of eyes glinted in the yellow light.

"Is someone else here?" I asked.

"Amr's little sister. I let him bring her along. Make yourself comfortable, abu khoaga. Do you want tea?"

"I do."

Ramzi turned on the boiler and I meanwhile lit a cigarette and sat on the floor. Amr and his sister, who was around seven or eight, barefoot and dirty, sat in view of us, eating the kusherie together.

Ramzi handed me the tea in a grimy metal mug. I took a sip. It was nauseatingly sweet.

"Your boy?" I asked.

"No way."

"Then?"

"Son of a dog."

In Cairo, that's what they call the city's innumerable street children.

"I said he could stay here as long as he keeps brawling well."

"Do you pay him?"

"He gets 500 geneihs after every win."

"And how much do you make?"

"That's none of your business," he said, capping it off with coughing laughter.

I took a drag on my cigarette. My forehead was throbbing from the insomnia.

"Where is the opium?" I asked.

"Here it is already," Ramzi replied. "Don't be getting impatient." Reaching into his djellaba, he fished out a package wrapped in perspiring brown paper. The smell struck my nose at once. He tore off a chunk and pressed it into my hand, and I rolled the opium into a ball. It was tart, but I knew everything would be better quickly now.

"Sweet dreams, abu khoaga," Ramzi said as he lay down on the sofa.

Pressing my back against the wall, I lit another cigarette and waited.

First my tongue went numb. It went numb and disappeared, as if it had never existed. No longer did I need to form words with it, for it had vanished without a trace. This was followed by my legs, which I no longer needed, and my hands, which I'd cursed a thousand times. My heart, which regularly pumped in a rage, quieted now. Its purring calmed me. Time ceased.

No longer did sweat form puddles on my skin, and the fine yellow dust sifting this way from the desert, which colored and sickened the palm trees in the yard, froze in the air. The stones in this forest of stones no longer crackled. The black hearses stopped on the access road.

In my dream I see a woman. A white-skinned brunette. Her eyes are a fire ablaze, glowing-hot brass in a smelter.

She is standing on a dune. The sand sinks under her feet, the wind blows her white dress. The brilliance of day glows behind her, yet it is night. The light hurts my eyes.

I stand at the foot of the dune and, driven by an inexpressible force, charge toward her, up to my knees in the hot sand, which burns my legs. I call out, but she does not hear. She turns with her face toward the night. In vain I implore her to help me. She doesn't even look; she doesn't hear my voice.

Years pass, it seems, by the time I reach the top. Both of my legs are scorched red. As I approach the woman, my strength leaves me. I lie prostrate. But I don't need strength to take in the view. All of the light is from a burning city. Apartment blocks are ablaze, factories are ablaze, grocery stores are ablaze, bus stops are ablaze. The geraniums in the windows, they too are ablaze, as are the parks. Even the ground is burning with yellow flames. The smoke is suffocating. Greasy ash rises in a dense plume before falling in light flakes, daubing my face and hands.

The woe that takes hold of me as I watch is different from any I've felt until now. It is the sadness of someone who has lost everything he's known and loved.

"Who did this?" I ask.

A black cloud rises beside the city. Soot? No, for the cloud changes direction and heads my way. It is a flock of crows. Their incessant cawing muffles the sound of the fire.

Until now the woman has stood with her back to me, looking into the night. She turns and opens her fist, and something falls out, twirling down into the sand: a blue plastic lighter of the sort available in any shop. The moment it hits the ground, it bursts into flame.

"Why?" I ask, hunched up.

I try taking hold of her leg, but my hand passes through. I get up on my knees and then to my feet. The crows circle above, so close I can see the feathers on their extended wings.

"Why did you do it?" I ask again. The irises disappear from her eyes, leaving them as white as the moon. With slow steps she heads down the hill.

A voice reminiscent of a raging river bellows: "Everything is valid—you can do anything."

The city, which just before was burning in one big flame behind me, is silent and still. I run down the slope, thinking I might find something to save in the charred ruins. For hours I poke through the debris, but nothing. I am set to give up when I find, in one of the mangled heaps, a board bearing this inscription:

"Not believing in a thing is a great freedom."

My teeth are chattering, my hands are trembling. I can see my breath.

"Just keep practicing," someone said.

I felt the sun against my skin, the light penetrating my closed eyelids.

"I don't want to."

"Come on, give it one more try. It's not so hard. See?"

I opened my eyes. I was inside the crypt. My lips were parched. I took out a cigarette and lit up.

"I don't want to do this," the little girl said again. She was sitting on the ground in the yard in front of a colored drill-book. Amr leaned over her. Her upper body was bare, her bones pressing visibly against her skin.

"You've got to do it, you've got to learn how to write."

"Why? You can't write."

"Exactly. So you don't turn out as dumb as your older brother."

"And so I can teach you."

"Yes."

A coughing fit took hold of me. Both of them turned. The little girl stared in shock. She began wildly scratching at her dreadlocks.

"Don't be scared, Emira," said Amr. "The man is a friend of Mr. Ramzi."

"Good morning, sir."

"Good morning. Don't call me 'sir,' Amr. My name is Daniel."

"Good morning, Mr. Daniel."

"Where is Ramzi?"

"He asked me to tell you he's waiting in the café."

"Where is that?"

"Three streets from here."

"Can you lead me?" I asked.

I stepped to the plastic barrel in which Ramzi kept water for washing up, and, using the mess tin tied to its side, ladled some over my head. It soaked my shirt and washed the remains of the opium out of me.

The City of the Dead was alive and breathing. Men sat by the gates of the dilapidated burial chambers, children scampered about on the muddy dirt road. Wafting through the air, the sickly-sweet smell of decomposition.

"How old are you, boy?" I asked Amr.

"I don't know, sir."

"How is it that you don't know?"

"I don't know."

"Do you know when you were born?"

"No, sir."

"Where are your parents?"

"Our mother died. I don't know about our father."

I tried keeping pace with him, and for a while we fell silent. Dehydration had left me dizzy, so we stopped at a grimy kiosk where I bought a big bottle of water and a chocolate bar. I drank half the water in one gulp, then pressed the bottle into the boy's hand. I gave him half the chocolate also. He gobbled it up and smiled.

"You're a really good man, sir," he said.

"Where did you get that idea?"

"You're a friend of Mr. Ramzi. And Mr. Ramzi is a really good man."

From the alleyway we arrived at a wider road. That's where the café was. Fashioned out of a garage, it had plastic tables in front and was packed with men smoking hookahs and gesticulating ardently. Ramzi was at a table with two of them. He waved. Amr accompanied me to the table and courteously greeted the others, who returned the greeting. He then spoke.

"Mr. Ramzi, if you don't need me, I would go back to the house."

Ramzi signaled with a wave that he could go.

"Sit down, *abu khoaga*," Ramzi said, pointing to an empty chair. "These gentlemen are Mohamed Gamal and Mustafa Abdelkader. They have an interest in the matches."

"Ahlan," said the men, who immediately resumed their conversation.

"I say you should face him off against the Palestinian all the same," said the one called Mohamed Gamal.

"It's too early yet," said Ramzi. "I need one more win."

"You won't find anyone. The little lion has a reputation."

"Not as big as the Palestinian's."

"The Palestinian will eat him for breakfast."

For a moment they pondered in silence.

"Abdelkader, isn't your boy fighting today?" Ramzi asked the other.

"Well, there are no plans."

"And don't you want to make a plan?"

"For two thousand geneihs, yes."

"Make it five hundred geneihs."

"You don't have a mother, Ramzi."

Ramzi broke into a grin.

"Nor a father. A thousand, but not one more."

"You were borne by dogs, like sin. A thousand two hundred."

"A thousand two hundred."

They shook hands, whereupon Ramzi counted 1,200 pounds into the man's hands. Abdelkader gave a whistle. A young street kid ran up to him. Abdelkader whispered something in his ear, and the child ran on.

"It will be proclaimed," he said, and then stood from the table and shook hands with us. Mohamed Gamal followed him. I remained alone with Ramzi.

He took a sip of his tea and grinned. "How did you sleep, abu khoaga?"

"I slept."

"Did you dream?"

"Yes."

"Don't take these dreams seriously and don't dwell on them."

"Why?"

"Because these dreams are from the devil."

"I don't believe in the devil."

"But it's in these dreams that the devil tells you how he sees you." He laughed. He lit a cigarette and waved over the café's waiter. "What are you drinking?"

"Coffee."

The waiter nodded, and shouted back to the shed where the stove was.

"Any news about the Bedouins?" I asked.

"Nothing yet. They always come on the weekend."

I too lit a cigarette. The waiter brought a coffee. I leaned back in the chair and stared at the street. Not far from the café a group of rugged-faced old women sat on little chairs, killing chickens. They took the birds out of wooden cages, cut their throats with well-practiced motions, and let the blood drain to the ground. It gathered in a big puddle all around their feet and flowed with the sludge down the street. The sun flashed against their kitchen knives, blinding me momentarily.

Opening my eyes, I saw my boy's mother, barefoot, in a miniskirt, taking little steps beside the old women, holding our son's hand. She was smiling as the blood colored her foot up till her ankle. I shook my head, and when I looked their way again, they were gone. Those few seconds had me late in noticing the two boys, street children, stepping over to the table. In torn slippers, shorts, and dirty, ad-emblazoned T-shirts they stood beside our table. The older one spoke.

"Mr. Ramzi, I can punch like a rocket."

"Yes," Ramzi said, knitting his brows.

"Yes," the boy repeated. "Like a rocket."

To prove his point, with full force he punched the kid standing beside him. The kid hurled ten feet backwards and landed face up on the ground. The scene elicited general mirth in the café.

"I can knock out anyone," the boy said, while his companion got up slowly, dusted himself off, and stepped back to the table.

Ramzi hemmed and hawed. "That's your friend?" he asked, pointing to the younger one.

"Yes."

"I want you to hit Rocket with all of your might."

"But why?"

"Because anyone can hit. The big thing is to endure the blows."

"Go ahead and hit me," said Rocket.

"I don't want to," replied the younger boy.

"Hit me," Rocket insisted, closing his eyes.

The younger boy looked around, took a step back, and put his weight on his right foot.

"Hit me already."

He hit with full force, catching Rocket on the jaw. The blow spun him before he crumpled to the ground. Blood dribbled from his nose.

For the half a minute Rocket lay unconscious, the younger boy slapped him so he would come to.

"Get out of my sight," Ramzi said once he stopped laughing. Their heads down, the two boys vanished into the alleyway.

"Is this how you picked up Amr?" I asked. "Did he apply as well?"

"Of course not. True gems are found in boulders, not at the market."

"How did you find him, then?"

"By chance. I was heading home from the Bahtak, where I'd been to bet, when I spotted a baltagiya gang, eight of them, taking money on the street. One of them got the hots for Amr's little sister."

"And?"

"They held a knife close to her eyes to show who she belonged to. That's what they tend to do."

"And?"

"Well, I started watching them rip the clothes off the little girl. They had no idea what they'd gotten themselves into."

"Amr showed up."

"He struck down three of the kids at once. The rest gave him a hell of a beating. They hit him with sticks, and when they thought Amr wouldn't be getting up anymore, they turned their attention back to the girl."

"But Amr got up."

"Yes. I think he even killed one of them, since that kid didn't get up as long as we were there. So, I went over, struck two of them on the head with a board, and when the rest of them ran off, I asked if he wanted to work for me."

"When was that?"

"About two months ago. They didn't have a place to sleep, so I let them into my place. What can I say? The boy's earned his keep. So far no one's beaten him, and we're through twelve bouts already. Soon he'll pass the Palestinian's record. Well then, let's go, abu khoaga. I'd ask you to let Amr know he'll be fighting today, too. I'll go off and make sure everyone in Arafa knows about it."

"Aren't you worried the police will come?"

"I hope they do. They place the biggest bets."

We stood from the table. Ramzi headed left, and I went the other way, back toward his place.

In the inner yard of the crypt, Amr's sister was shouting through her sobs, "Cut it off, cut it off already!" In her hands was a pair of scissors she was trying to press into her big brother's hands, but he did not take them.

"You're a girl. What will people say if I cut off your hair?"

The little girl flung the scissors to the ground and ran inside.

"Did you know there's a match tonight?" I said, turning to Amr.

"Yes, sir," he said.

I went into the room where I'd slept, sat against the wall, lit up a cigarette, and looked out of my head.

Ramzi got back around five. He came in and sat across from me on the floor, opened a plastic bag of kusherie, and began spooning it out.

"Do you want some?" he asked.

"I'm not hungry."

"They're betting for the boy three to one," he said, his mouth full.

"Are you happy about that"

"It's not so good. Soon there won't be anyone to take him on."

He shouted out to the yard, and Amr appeared in the doorway.

"At your service, Mr. Ramzi."

"Sit down. Abu khoaga has of course already told you that you'll be fighting tonight."

"Yes, sir."

"Abdelkader's boy is good. I've seen him fight."

"I know him, sir."

"Can you beat him?"

"Yes, sir."

"I've got a lot of money on this fight."

"Don't you worry, sir. I won't disappoint you."

"Fine, then. Go and get ready."

The sun was setting behind the Mokattam Hills. The boulders were red, the sky was red, the starlings zigzagging among the houses were red. Amr was running in place beside me to warm up his muscles. We didn't talk. I watched the ground under my feet, the sewage-swollen mud. The locals burned trash at the end of the road, and the air was heavy with the smell of burning plastic.

We turned left, down the alleyway leading to the Bahtak. Two mongrels were again hanging from the walls. Fresh kills.

"Why do they hang dogs?" I asked Amr.

"Because it's custom."

People were gathering on the square, and the usual oil barrels had already been set up to create the ring. Ramzi waved to us from the other side of the square.

"You got here just in time."

"What happens next?" I asked Ramzi.

"Soon they'll signal that the betting will begin. Meanwhile the boys will stand in among the barrels. Can I ask you for a favor, abu khoaga?" Ramzi pulled rolls of tape and sterile gauze from his pocket. "Would you put the bandages on Amr while I go around and talk with those I've bet with?"

I waved to Amr for us to stand off to the side. Amr took off his T-shirt, deferentially extended his arm, and I began to wrap the gauze.

"Aren't you anxious?" I asked. We were next to a burning heap of trash, its sparks occasionally coming close as I worked.

"No, sir," he replied.

"Not even a little?"

"No, sir. I wasn't born to be beaten."

I stopped wrapping.

"Then what were you born for?"

"I don't know that. All I know is what I wasn't born for."

"That isn't bad for a start."

Having finished with his right hand, I took out my switchblade and used it to cut a length of tape.

"May I ask something, sir?"

"Ask."

"What are you doing here?"

"I don't know. I have time."

"You don't belong here."

"That's not certain."

"But it is, completely certain. Don't you have a family?"

"I did," I said, and finished his left hand.

"What happened to them?"

"They died. Now go."

Amr headed off, slipping between the oil barrels and stopping in the middle of the ring. The crowd got boisterous, some people clapping and others shrieking as married women did at weddings. Finally, the other boy, too, got in the ring. He was just as tall as Amr, but a good bit heavier. One look at his arms made it clear he was used to manual labor. The two children stood side by side, not even looking at each other while the betting was underway. For several long minutes they stood there without a word, and then a silver-haired old man with crooked teeth, using the same board that had signaled the start of the betting, once again hit one of the barrels. The onlookers fell silent.

"May Allah decide which of you is better," the old man said. The two children locked eyes and began to circle each other.

The pudgy boy swung his right hand. Amr dodged it and replied at once. His left hand cracked against the boy's forehead. The crowd raved. Though Amr's punch was by no means strong, the other boy was clearly consumed by rage. He charged at Amr. The momentum sent both of them into a barrel, which lurched and tilted until the crowd set it back in place along with the fighters. The pudgy boy pummeled Amr's chest with both hands. He got in at least six blows before Amr drove an elbow full-force into his nose, sending him flying out of the corner, blood flowing from his nostrils.

"That's my boy!" Ramzi howled.

Turning toward him, Amr raised his hands in the air.

He heard the crowd's cautionary murmurs too late. The pudgy boy, taking advantage of his distraction, grabbed a wooden board from among the barrels and struck Amr in the side so hard the board broke off in his hand. Amr fell, pressing a hand to his side, and spat blood. By now the crowd was hooting, some people flinging rocks and trash at the pudgy boy, who dropped the stump of the board and shouted, "Stand up!"

When Amr got to his feet, the crowd fell silent.

Someone called out, "Kill him, Little Lion!"

The pudgy boy rushed at Amr and began to pummel his torso again. Pressing his left hand to his side, Amr took a couple of uncertain steps backwards and tried to defend himself one-handed, but pain showed in his eyes with every blow. At a lucky moment, he managed to shove the pudgy boy, just enough for him to lose his balance and fall, and Amr didn't hesitate. He fired away with precise, mighty blows.

"My boy!" Ramzi howled through a mouthful of food, and with a self-satisfied grin he set off to collect from those who'd placed bets. Amr silently climbed out of the ring, and when he saw me, he came my way, extending his hands to have me cut off the bandages. I took out my knife and was snipping the gauze around his left hand when I noticed the suffusion of blood under his skin. A dark bruise covered the whole of his left side.

"Does it hurt when you take a breath?" I asked.

"A little."

"A couple of your ribs might be broken."

As I finished with his right hand, Ramzi appeared with a wide grin and a fat wad of hundred-geneih notes. He was ecstatic.

"This is yours, boy," he said, counting out seven of them.

Amr was wide-eyed. "But this is two hundred pounds more than what we agreed on, sir."

"No problem, you deserve it. You fought like a lion."

"You are really generous, sir. I really thank you for what you do for me."

"Abu khoaga, tonight we're celebrating!"

"Did the Bedouins arrive?"

"Not yet, but this was a good day."

He stopped at a food stand, shouted inside, and ordered a kilogram of koftas and rice. By the time we got back to the crypt, it had already been delivered.

We sat in the big room, on the floor, eating. Ramzi was in a jubilant mood. He put meat, salad, and rice on a plastic plate and called to Amr to give it to his sister. I wasn't hungry. I just poked at mine.

"Abu khoaga, you are already waiting for Abu Salam," Ramzi said through a grin.

"What was that?"

"For the father of peace."

"Yes," I said, realizing he meant the opium.

"And here you are," he said, removing from his djellaba the plastic bag in which he kept his personal supply. He took out a bit and put it in my hand. I stared at the moist, red lump before placing it under my tongue.

Ramzi turned to Amr. "Do you want some?"

The boy stood up and immediately pressed a hand to his side. "What, sir?"

"Opium. It brings lovely dreams."

He held the bag toward Amr, but I pushed his arm aside.

"You don't need this, boy," I said.

"Why wouldn't he?" Ramzi asked, smirking.

"Because it's those who don't have dreams who eat this."

I climb toward a tent encampment under the Milky Way, the stars glimmering above me like milk spilled on black fabric.

A gypsy encampment, I think on noticing the tents. The sort one still sees in the rural reaches of Eastern Europe. Carnival carts piled high with bric-a-brac and human beings. But they are not wandering. The tents are staked, the tarps stretched tight.

Over tamped-down earth I walk toward the camp. Millennia have passed since I heard a human voice. But if I encounter people here, it's possible they will be nothing but shadows of who they were before moving into the desert. Now they savor the nighttime music of the jackals.

There's a blazing fire in the middle of the encampment, flames shooting high, two women in the light, dancing around the fire, tambourines in their hands, bells on their feet. Light gathers in their naked navels.

"You did come, after all," they say on seeing me, their bodies still shaking about.

"We've been waiting for you," say toothless old people from the shadows as I reach the fire.

"Why?" I ask.

"Because you have business here."

"What sort?"

The two dancing girls smile and wave their hands for me to follow. We come upon a chasm at the edge of the hill. It is deep and seemingly bottomless, like despair. I am not alone here, at this precipice, but surrounded by faces from several nations, people flinging their belongings over the edge. I have nothing to say. The two girls don't stop dancing for even a moment. They beat their tambourines and drum with their feet. As I watch, cold sweat draws patterns on my back.

The girls turn to me and smile, revealing their gold teeth.

"Now it's your turn," they say. "The time has come."

A wizened man steps forward, holding a small child, which he hands to me.

"Who is this?" I ask.

"He's dead," they say. "And if he's not, throw him down all the same. You can't do anything for him anyway."

I gaze at the blond boy asleep in my hands. Or was he really dead? If I throw him away, I really won't have anything left.

"If you don't," says the old man, "you'll be the one plummeting into the dark."

The sand grated between my teeth. I lay on my belly, my face buried in the filthy mattress. I was parched. I reached into my pocket to check the time on my phone—it had lost its charge.

I stood up. My trousers sloshed about on me. Since this insomnia began, I'd lost nearly a quarter of my weight.

Nothing was stirring in the yard. I lit a cigarette, sat on the ground, dizzy. I thought, *Life is actually wonderful as long as you can sleep normally.* A green carrion-fly landed on my hand and rubbed its legs together. A clanking roused me from my thoughts. Someone was pounding at the metal gate. I couldn't see a thing from where I sat and hadn't the slightest intention of opening it. No one would be looking for me here.

Whoever it was kept pounding until Amr emerged. He was shirtless, a huge purple splotch on his side. He took slow, measured steps, drew the latch, and pulled the door wide open. It was Mohamed Gamal, from the café yesterday.

"*Assalamu Aleykum Arrahmatulla*," Gamal said.

"*Va Alaykum salam*," said Amr. "Mr. Ramzi isn't home."

"No problem. In fact it's you I'm looking for, Little Lion. May I come in?"

Amr opened the door even wider.

"Come, let's sit down," Gamal said, taking out a cigarette. "Want one?"

"I don't smoke, sir."

"That's good. It's not healthy."

He put the cigarette in his mouth and lit it. I could hear the tobacco frizzling. For a few moments they sat beside each other in silence.

"You know, the Palestinian is my man."

"I know."

"Soon he'll be taken away to the army. I'd like you to come over to me, fight for me. You could be the champion of all of Araf. I'd pay you very well."

"I fight for Mr. Ramzi."

"I don't know how much Ramzi pays you, but I'll double it."

"It's not about money. He saved our lives."

"Oh, come now. Ramzi is a scoundrel. He doesn't do a thing out of the kindness of his heart."

"Get out of here, sir," Amr said, standing up. Gamal followed.

"You don't get it. If you don't work for me, you'll have to take on the Palestinian, who will kill you. I'll make sure of that."

"Get out."

Gamal turned around on the street. "I'll be laughing my head off as I watch you drowning in your own blood, you little shit."

Amr locked the gate and headed back. I could hear his sister whimpering inside their hovel of a room.

"I don't want you to die and drown in your own blood," she said through tears.

"No one will kill me, Emira, don't be scared. Allah won't allow it."

I stepped over to the barrel to wash off, but as I dipped the watering can and lifted it out, the world spun around me. I have no idea how long I was out, but on coming to I saw Amr leaning above me, wiping my face with a wet rag.

"Are you all right, sir?" he asked. "I thought you had gone with Mr. Ramzi."

"I was sleeping," I said. "I forgot to eat, that's all. I need to eat something."

I sat up, then stood. The dizziness had not passed. "I'm off for some food," I said.

Amr nodded.

"How is your side?" I asked.

"It hurts. Especially when I move."

"It'll be better in a week or two."

"Inshallah."

I stumbled through the gate and down the alleyway, all the way to the first food stand, where workers were frying falafels in a huge pan. The oil was dark brown. I asked for two geneihs' worth, and the clerk wrapped them in newspaper. Forcing myself, I took the first falafel into my mouth, chewed it, and swallowed. I thought I would throw it up.

I walked down the street eating, telling myself with each bite, *If you don't eat, you will die.* At the café, I ordered a coffee. It felt surprisingly good.

As I sat there, a street kid stopped at every crypt, garage, and food stand, shouting, "Tonight, Palestinian the Terrible will return to the Bahtak to score a victory! After the Isha prayer he will finish off his victim." When he was reassured that everyone had heard him, he moved on. I took a drag on my cigarette and signaled for another coffee.

Before long, Ramzi appeared at the other end of the alleyway. He seemed careworn as he shuffled along, his hands in the pockets of his djellaba.

"Master Ramzi," I said.

"Abu khoaga," he replied, and sat down in the chair opposite mine.

"I've heard the Palestinian will fight tonight."

"Yes, they brought a boy for him from Shubra, since no one in Arafa will take him on. Mohamed Gamal, whom he is fighting for, has offered a fortune for Amr to go up against him tomorrow."

"He's that good?"

"He is. And he shows no mercy to anyone."

"Amr was injured in the last bout."

"I know. But it's not so simple. Gamal was completely beside himself when I refused."

"Why?"

"I figure he's taking it badly when folks say Amr will be the next champion. He says it would be best if I reconsider while he is being nice about it."

"What did you say to that?"

"That I would think about it. He offered lots of money."

When we reached home, Amr and his sister were sitting in the yard, again practicing reading. Lost in thought, Ramzi smoked while I lay on the mattress.

Two hours passed before Ramzi spoke.

"Tomorrow you've got to fight, Amr. I didn't want it, but I have no choice."

"I understand, sir."

"Mohamed Gamal is an influential man. And the police chief's nephew. It's not good to snub him."

"Yes."

"You wouldn't want the cops to take you away."

"No, sir."

"So you can fight?"

"Yes, sir. I will win. I won't let you down."

"Fine, then."

I stood and went into the yard. Ramzi looked at me. "I have no choice," he said.

I went to the barrel, ladled out some water, and washed my face.

Ramzi wanted to go to the Bahtak to talk with Mohamed Gamal. I went with him. A big crowd had already gathered on the square; lots of people wanted to see the Palestinian. Separated from Ramzi, I cut across the square and leaned my back against the alley wall. I could see everything from there. The fighters were not yet in the ring, but dozens of men were placing bets with the bookmakers, who were easy to spot because they had big wads of cash in their hands. In the cacophony I could just make out that they were betting 5:1 for the Palestinian.

I lit up and stared at the crowd. Ramzi was across the square, nervously gesticulating at Mohamed Gamal and two other men. Gamal raised his hands several times to calm him down. After a while they shook hands and slapped each other's backs. Gamal headed to the ring, and the first boy entered, sinewy and of medium build, wearing blue sweatpants.

"Is this the Palestinian?" I asked the middle-aged man beside me.

"No," he replied. "This is just the kid from Shubra. That there is the Palestinian."

A tall, sixteenish boy stepped in among the barrels. His skin was shockingly light, almost as white as mine. He was bald, and his face was disfigured by deep scars that made him look as if he was snarling. It was written all over him that he'd seen a lot in his young life.

"Is he really Palestinian?" I asked.

"From Rafah, in the Gaza Strip. His parents were killed by the Jews, but the devil saved him. At twelve he came alone to Cairo and the dogs didn't gobble him up. He gobbled up the dogs."

The kid from Shubra was jogging in place and shadowboxing. The Palestinian slowly circled him while also punching the air as the betting went on.

When the same old man as last time announced the start of the match, the two children stood face to face. The Palestinian raised his hands to protect his head as the kid from Shubra moved in. Several times, though, the kid struck nothing but air, since the Palestinian kept dodging his blows, practically dancing among the barrels. He knew how to fight. For several long minutes he toyed with the kid from Shubra. Then, once the other began to slow down and was clearly out of breath, the Palestinian stopped and leveled a single blow, a faultless right hook.

A beautiful blow it was; I could hear his nose crack. The kid was on the ground at once, the crowd raving.

"That's all?" shouted the Palestinian, spitting on him. "What did you bring me? A lamb?"

"You show him!" people called from the crowd. "Show him!"

"Stand up already!" The Palestinian leaned down and, grabbing the boy by the hair, yanked him to his feet. Blood was flowing from his nostrils and he wasn't completely conscious.

"You thought you'd come here and take what's mine?" the Palestinian asked, screaming it so everyone could hear.

"That's what he thought!" the crowd shouted.

"You were badly mistaken!" said the Palestinian, striking the boy's face again, sprawling him into the mud. The boy crawled toward the edge of the ring. The Palestinian stood still at first, celebrating himself. Only when the boy reached the barrels did he intervene.

"And just where are you going?" he shouted, grabbing the boy by the right leg and pulling him back to the middle. The boy gave a kick. It caught the Palestinian's thigh, but it wasn't strong.

"What do they do with sheep around here?" the Palestinian asked.

"They cut their throats!" screamed the wild crowd.

"Exactly!" the Palestinian cried, and jumped on the boy's chest.

Surely ribs splintered under the weight. From the outside, though, all we could see was the boy lying helplessly on the ground, grimy with dirt and his own blood.

The Palestinian kept jumping on the boy's chest. "Get this lamb out of my sight!"

The crowd went wild. They took the Palestinian on their shoulders and carried him around the square. For some twenty minutes they raved and cheered away. The boy from Shubra lay in the ring just as the Palestinian had left him. An hour passed by before the crowd calmed enough for the bookmakers to start paying out. The boy had not come to.

"I think he killed that kid," I said to Ramzi on the way home.

"Yep," Ramzi replied and spat on the ground.

I am going to die, *I think as I charge through the sand. I free my right foot and take one step upward. That step, too, sees my foot sink, but by putting my weight on it I am able to free the other. And so I go on, ascending the hill.*

It is scorching hot, the air choked with fine grains of sand. Everything is the color of sand, even the sun. The wind is strong but it brings no relief. It burns like red-hot steel, and the gusting sand scratches at my skin. For several hours I've been trudging up and down hills to reach the city that I glimpse from the summits. Will I ever get there? I've been walking for half a day and seem no closer. I lost time somewhere back in Alexandria. Maybe in the Tugaria Café, on the Corniche, after breakfast, when I was reading the papers and the cardamom was still stinging my tongue. I might have lost it by the diesel-smelling fisherman as he wrapped squid in yesterday's papers. Or perhaps at the sandy beach of the Greek club, Omilos, along with my lifetime membership, as I drank light beer under the blue-and-white striped parasol. Nor is it out of the question that she took it along with the child. It got into the suitcase while packing, between two diapers and the baby food.

The point is I'd lost time and sought after it in vain. No one has returned it. Since then it has always been just now. So I don't know exactly when I first heard the words "I am going to die." It might have been at the foot of some hill as I prepared to ascend. It would be an hour at most before I'd find myself standing in the kitchen of my own home, letting water run from the tap.

I'm going to die, *I think at the foot of the hill.*

One more hour, *I reply, dragging myself further.*

I've just reached the top when my legs can no longer move. I collapse. My head hits the ground with a thud. I know it's over. I wait for my heart to stop.

There are no clouds in the sky to help me guess at the passing of time. The sun does not move from its place. At some point I notice a figure wobbling at the foot of the hill. It seems as if I'm hallucinating from dehydration, but the figure keeps approaching. He looks like a child, with small hands and small feet. Only his eyes and face reveal him to be old. He is leading a donkey just as little as he is.

"You are exhausted," he says, grinning at me.

"Leave me alone."

"That cannot be done."

"I want this whole thing to end."

"You really think it matters what you want?"'

The dwarf takes various tools from a bag affixed to the donkey's side. He leans toward me and rips open my shirt.

"Leave me alone, please."

"I'm afraid that isn't possible," he replies with a whistle while examining my chest. "I'm not the one who sets the rules . . . What do you know, found it already!"

With a yank he pulls open the skin of my chest. Underneath—where there should be lungs, a heart, muscles—there is instead a complex mechanical structure. Interconnected cogs by the thousands turn and hiss. The dwarf locates a key in his pocket and places it in a hole. It fits perfectly. He winds counterclockwise, with an expert hand.

"And we're all set," he says, whistling calmly as he puts his tools back in his bag and heads down the hill.

"Who are you?"

He exclaims in return: "Who are you?"

I sat in the yard of the crypt, a couple of minutes past noon, waiting for my heart to beat the opium out of it. The day was unbearably hot; what little wind there was, was blowing from the Mokattam Hills, scattering fine dust over the City of the Dead. I looked at the wash hanging out to dry. Faded, stretched T-shirts, sweatpants, and djellabas, water dripping on the ground.

Amr was doing the laundry.

The boy crouched in front of two plastic vats, rubbing clothes with detergent in one, rinsing them in the other, then hanging them to dry. For a long time, I watched him work. He was bare from the waist up, his sides purple, his ribs pressing against the skin. He was emptying one of the vats in the dirt when the iron gate squeaked open. Ramzi was returning from the street, a black plastic bag in his hand.

"So, you've woken up, abu khoaga." He sat beside me and took a sandwich from the bag. "Want some?"

"No."

"Hey, Amr!" he shouted, throwing the bag to the boy, who caught it and looked back with gratitude.

"Thank you, sir," he said, and went inside his space.

For a while Ramzi ate in silence beside me.

"They're betting seven to one against Amr," he said.

"After yesterday's bout I'm not surprised," I replied.

"Do you think he'll lose?"

"I don't know. The Palestinian learned to fight. And Amr's side hurts."

"Amr fights well, too."

"When he's not injured."

Ramzi reached over with a cigarette. We had a smoke.

"Excuse me, sirs," Amr said, emerging from his room, "but I heard what you were talking about." He paused. "Would you allow me to say something. Mr. Ramzi?"

"Sure, boy."

"Don't worry about the bets. I will win tonight's match."

"What makes you think that?" I asked.

"All the Palestinian can do is hit. If I get close to him he won't be able to do a thing."

"Have you seen him fight before?"

Amr nodded, then turned to Ramzi. "Bet on me, sir. You can win lots of money with that, and I can maybe show my gratitude for your kindness."

Ramzi nodded and stood up. "I'm off to take care of it." From the gate he called back to the boy. "You don't owe me anything, by the way."

After Ramzi left, I remained alone with Amr.

"Did you really see the Palestinian fight?"

"Yes, sir, I saw three matches. If I can pull him to the ground, I can beat him."

"And if you can't?"

"I can, sir."

"How can you be so sure about this?"

"Because I'm fighting for something."

"For what?"

"For this," he said, waving his hand around the crypt.

We went out to the Bahtak early, walking beside each other in silence. The sun was still up and blazing strong.

The square was completely empty; only the barrels indicated where matches were held. With Amr I sat in front of one of the garages. We stared at an old color TV as six grimy Egyptians repaired a black Lada inside. There was neither nervousness nor tension on Amr's face.

"Where you came from, sir," Amr said, pointing at the TV, "is life really like this?"

"In a few places."

We fell silent.

"Why don't you take your little sister and leave while you can? The Palestinian will kill you."

"Don't you worry, sir. There won't be any trouble. Besides, where would we go?"

He turned his attention back to the movie. I watched the empty square, the rusty barrels, the adobe walls charred by the burning trash. An hour must have passed this way. The sun was setting fast by the time I noticed the old man who opened the matches appear at the end of one of the alleyways. He was dragging two slight-framed mongrels by the cords around their necks. The animals were resisting. The old man pulled them all the way to the barrels and there let go of the wire cord and stepped on it. Tails between their legs, the dogs whined and gasped for breath, trying in vain to escape. The man reached beside the barrels and pulled out an iron rod. The animals became frantic. He swung four or five times. Silence. Then the man came toward us, stopped beside me, and called in to the garage.

"Can I take your ladder, Ibrahim?"

"Take it."

He stepped into the garage and got a battered aluminum ladder from the corner, put it on his shoulder, and carried it to the dogs. Noticing Amr, he smirked. He picked up the carcasses and stood the ladder by the alleyway entrance. The sun set behind the Mokattam Hills and the trash heaps were set alight. The two dog carcasses dangled in the wind. The flames from the burning trash cast a huge black shadow that danced on the sooty walls of the square.

A crowd gathered on the Bahtak, people pressed against each other so tight you could hardly walk. Once again Ramzi handed me the roll of gauze and went to arrange the bets. Yesterday's fight had brought lots of takers.

I waited for the boy in a corner, not far from the barrels. Fifteen minutes later he turned up, a plastic container in his hands. He was spreading something all over himself with fierce determination. I figured it was some sort of oil, and when he got close to me, I smelled the sesame. His chest and hands sparkled in the firelight.

"Are you ready?" I asked.

"Yes."

"We can begin."

"*Allahu akbar*," Amr replied with a nod.

I bandaged his hands quickly. I took care to make the wrapping neither too tight nor so loose the gauze would slip off.

"Be careful," I said.

He nodded and sidled his way through the crowd. When he reached the ring, the audience began to rave. They smelled blood. The noise crescendoed when the Palestinian arrived. The old man had to pound the barrel several times to get everyone quiet. The two boys faced each other. For several long seconds they stared wordlessly.

"What are you waiting for?" someone shouted.

"Kill him, Palestinian!"

The Palestinian opened his harelip in a grin and raised his hand to his neck to signal that he would now kill Amr. He then jumped around him. Amr moved in sync. The Palestinian took jabs that Amr dodged or blocked.

"Come on already," the Palestinian yelled, but he could not unnerve Amr.

I found Ramzi and stood beside him. We watched the match in silence.

Both kids were taking rapid breaths, but there hadn't been a serious exchange. Again the Palestinian jabbed at Amr's head, but Amr dodged and hit right back. The punch wasn't serious, but it was enough to get blood flowing from the Palestinian's nose.

"Little Lion!" the crowd shrieked.

The Palestinian wiped his nose with his bandage, enraged. He charged, and though Amr raised his arm in defense, the fifth blow caught his upper body, right where the board had broken over him the day before. Blood spurted from his mouth. After three more blows to his ribs, Amr collapsed. The Palestinian knelt on his face and then, standing up, knocked his head against one of the barrels.

The crowd went wild, and this the Palestinian liked most of all.

"So, he's a Little Lion?" he asked.

"Kill him, Palestinian!"

Amr stood, pressing his hands to his ribs. Mud slid down his oily body. "Is that all you can do?" he asked.

The Palestinian ran at him and hit his head full force several times, the thuds resonating across the square. Amr was on the ground again.

Swimming in his own sweat, the Palestinian raised his hands triumphantly. "This is no lion, this is the son of a dog."

I turned toward Ramzi, who stood gazing silently. "This is butchery," I said. "Can you stop it?"

"Huh?" He cast me a look of incomprehension.

The crowd was screaming, "Kill him!"

"What do we do with dogs?" the Palestinian asked, passing his eyes over the people, and the crowd bellowed in reply, "Hang them! Choke them!"

Not wanting to see, I turned away. But everyone fell silent. I looked back, and Amr was standing again. His eyebrows were torn and one of his eyes was swollen shut, but he was upright. "Is that all you can do?" he asked.

The Palestinian rushed at him and pounded the boy's head. Again, Amr collapsed. The Palestinian went on kicking him until he had to lean against a barrel.

"So, stand up now, Little Lion," he said, gasping for air.

The crowd raved, then fell silent. Amr was up on his knees, and, wobbling, he staggered to his feet. The Palestinian stared at him in shock.

"Is that all?" Amr asked. His teeth were bloody. "Is that all you can do?"

Screaming, the Palestinian lunged. He hit Amr's face again and again, until he too collapsed.

"He's going to kill him," I said to Ramzi. "Stop this."

"I can't."

The Palestinian got off Amr and stumbled to one of the barrels. "Just get up now," he said, spitting on the ground. "Let's go."

Amr didn't move. I couldn't tell if he was breathing. The Palestinian panted for half a minute.

"Mongrels are beaten to death around here," he said. He raised one of the barrels over his head, and, as the crowd screamed on, he headed back to Amr. "Farewell, Little Lion."

Before he could throw the barrel, Amr struck the Palestinian's balls dead on. The barrel landed on the older boy's belly as he fell backwards.

Amr slowly got up and, stumbling along, went toward the Palestinian. He clutched the older boy's neck, then threw himself backwards to the ground, putting him in a chokehold. The Palestinian kicked out in vain. Amr went on clutching until finally the body stiffened, then slackened. The crowd stood numb.

Amr let go. At that, the crowd went wild. Amr, though, just sat in the mud, one hand pressed to his side. He'd gotten a hell of a beating. I jostled my way to the ring. On spotting me, Amr clambered out from among the barrels and put his hands around my neck. He couldn't hold himself up. I had to drag him as people slapped his back, wanting to touch the hero. Only when we reached the corner of the square was there space to sit down and remove his bandages.

"I won," he muttered into the air.

"You won," I echoed.

Ramzi came by an hour later, as the crowd was dispersing.

"Are we leaving?" he asked.

Amr nodded and, with my help, managed to stand.

"Was I good, sir?"

"Yes," Ramzi said. "It happened like you told us."

"Aren't you hungry?" I asked.

"Yes, sir," the boy replied. By now he was on his own feet.

"Fucking lion." Ramzi shook his head. "A fucking lion."

"That he is," I said.

We stopped at a food stand and bought sandwiches. Amr ate slowly. Suddenly he stopped, pressing a hand to his belly, and threw up, then fell over, unconscious. Both Ramzi and I jumped to help him. The boy's lips were purple, his skin gray. I slapped his cheeks lightly, but he didn't come to.

"He needs a hospital."

"Like hell he does," Ramzi said. "He's just exhausted. He'll sleep it out, and that will be all."

"He's bleeding inside. If we don't get him to a hospital, he'll die."

Ramzi looked at me. "Are you sure about that?"

"He threw up blood and he isn't coming to. He needs a hospital."

Ramzi looked hesitant. "Okay," he finally said. "There's a hospital by Sayeda Aisha. Help me lift him."

He gripped the boy under his arms while I held his legs, and that was how we went the length of the alleyway, out to the main road. It was packed. Vendors were selling their wares, and cars zigzagging around people, their headlights illuminating the fine dust swirling in the air. Finally a black Lada stopped and we sat Amr on the back seat. It took half an hour for the taxi to work past the muddy streets of the City of the Dead and reach the paved access road.

The Egyptian public hospital was a flat, sand-colored building with broken windows, grimy floors, and flickering neon lights. Ramzi paid the driver through the window and we lifted Amr out of the taxi and jostled our way through the crowd by the entrance. The receptionist—a fiftyish woman wearing a headscarf—sat beside an old, colonial-era office desk.

"He collapsed on the street," Ramzi said.

She looked us over. "You have to wait," she said.

We waited by a wall, Amr on the floor beside us. He was white as milk but still breathing. Twenty minutes passed before the doctor emerged. When he saw the child, he shouted. Nurses appeared and lay the boy on a stretcher, then rolled him into a room. Another twenty minutes went by before the doctor re-emerged, waving to Ramzi.

"Stay put," Ramzi told me. "It wouldn't be good if they saw a khoaga too. Your being there would jack up the price."

I stayed put. Ramzi spoke to the doctor for a long time. Meanwhile a woman screamed in the hallway. Her belly was huge. She kept invoking Allah and demanding that she be helped. I watched her face as contractions came and went.

Ramzi emerged anxious.

"What did the doctor say?"

"Broken ribs and a ruptured spleen. Internal bleeding. They're asking for a thousand pounds to operate."

I looked at him, waiting.

"I have five hundred pounds, abu khoaga. Don't you have five hundred?"

"No." I shook my head.

"Then we have to take him away from here. He won't survive that."

We looked at each other.

I said, "Wait here."

I went into the bathroom, whose floor squelched of piss. I stepped into one of the stalls and removed my right shoe. I took out the insole and, from underneath, my emergency reserve, wrapped in tissue. I counted it: four hundred fifty pounds. I put it in my pocket and went back to Ramzi.

"I have four hundred pounds."

"That'll do," he said. He took the money from my hand and returned to the room. This time he was back in five minutes.

"Has he come to?"

"No. Let's leave."

Without a word we headed out of the hospital, beating our way through the crowd by the entrance. We stopped by an overpass on the two-lane road, and for a while we stood beside each other in silence, smoking. Ramzi reached into his pocket and took out a plastic bag.

"Here is your opium, abu khoaga."

"Did the Bedouins come?"

"They did."

I slipped the bag into my pants pocket.

"Thank you."

"You're welcome."

I had no more reason to go with him, as we both knew.

"I'll be off now," he said, stepping on the remnant of his cigarette. He flagged down a cab and got in. "You can give me a ring anytime if you run out," he said, and gestured to the driver.

When the car reached the end of the road, it turned onto Sayeda Aisha Street. I held out my hand for another cab.

The Bluebird Hotel was just as I had left it. The elevator didn't have a door. The front desk clerk didn't look up from the soap opera he was watching, that was how he handed me the key. I had to shove the door to my room with my shoulders, since it was still stuck. In the shower, a week of dirt and grime washed off me into the drain. I plugged my phone into the charger, opened my knapsack, and removed two cans of warm beer.

Sooner or later I had to work, I knew, to pay for the room. But I felt too tired to start bombarding editors now. I stared at the vibrating monitor, smoked, and drank. It was 3 a.m., but I couldn't sleep.

Fuck it, I thought, and took out the raw opium. I set it in front of me on the table. I pinched off a larger portion than ever before, placed it under my tongue, and waited. When my mouth went numb, I clicked open the second can of beer and washed away the opium taste.

By the time I reach the top of the last hill, I know I've been going in circles. I am not far from where I set out, by the burned city. The view shows nothing but soot and debris. Charred ruins. Steel structures have opened like black flowers. Black rainwater gathers on black ground and flows into black canals.

Looking closer, I can see the woman's tracks and, further on, the arsonist herself as she trudges toward the city. She hasn't gotten far. She walks aimlessly, naked and wet, her hands pressed against her belly, in which she carries a child. Who impregnated her is a mystery, but the child will be very big. At the first ruins, she stumbles to a halt and cries out as her water breaks.

She takes deep breaths before moving on. I pick up my pace to keep from losing her. The ground is covered everywhere with thick, black ash, revealing her tracks. I pass the train station, charred black by the flames;

and then by the big park, where the trees' black branches stare blindly at the sky.

Following the sounds, I find her leaning against a tall pine, her legs wide apart. Her face contorts in pain, blood flowing between her legs. The convulsions are increasingly frequent. Finally, she squeezes something out of her womb. She faints and topples over.

She is not dead. I see her chest rise and fall as she breathes. And then I notice that what she pushed out is starting to stir. It is covered by a membrane or sac. It must be some kind of animal. Using claws, it tears through the membrane, and now I see what it is: a big, black dog, bloody and slimy. Its eyes shine red in the twilight.

I know what will happen. I stand still, but I can't watch. The sounds are enough. When the black dog finishes devouring her, not a bit is left. The dog's eyes flash red. It climbs onto one of the ruins, sniffs the air, and lumbers away.

I start after it, since I have no other choice. I will be following this beast as long as I live.

It was morning in Cairo. The sun lit up the Bluebird Hotel. Its light was warm and white, as always in the desert, anticipating the blazing hot afternoon.

I stared at the wall, which had been scribbled over with a pen. I shivered. Flies landed on my skin and bit, but I couldn't move. My head was throbbing, and my tongue was stuck to the roof of my mouth. Several long minutes passed this way.

Gathering strength, I felt around the bed for something drinkable. My fingers met with a half-full can of beer. I lifted it, trembling, but as the warm liquid reached my stomach, I retched.

Somehow I made it to the hotel's public toilet, which was across from my room.

For a long time, I heaved and spat, gripping the filthy pot with both hands. When the spasms ended, I staggered back to the room, sat on the edge of the bed, and forced the remaining beer down my throat.

Slowly, life came back into me. I knew who I was and what I'd done in recent days. I looked at my phone—the date and time told me I'd slept for forty-eight hours.

I remembered Amr and Ramzi, the bouts, and the City of the Dead. I turned on the phone and called Ramzi. It rang for a long time before he picked up.

"Abu khoaga. Don't tell me that what I gave is gone already."

"No."

"Because if it is, I can get as much for you as you want."

"How is Amr?"

A long silence ensued.

"Good," Ramzi said at last. "But you've got to see the new kid. A real champion. He hits like a rocket."

I put down the phone, stood up from the bed, and lit a cigarette. After showering, I made my way to the food stand across the street from the hotel.

I never looked up Ramzi again.

The Good Customer

"What will you have to drink?" I asked.

She was a tall, sinewy Sudanese woman in her early twenties. She wore a miniskirt, and her black hair flowed down onto her shoulders and framed her face and her brown eyes. I had to concentrate so as not to ogle her cleavage. Her nipples were hard, their contours evident under her dress. She was a black African woman, full of life.

We were in the Faris bar, in Ma'adi. Smoke hung in the air, and there was a crowd. Men and women, black and white, were drinking and smoking cigarettes, staring at the TV, whose volume was turned down, or awaiting their turn at the sole billiard table.

"A Stella," said the woman.

"Two Stellas," I shouted to the bar. The mustachioed Egyptian bartender leaned down to the fridge and took out two bottles of beer. He clicked off the caps and set the bottles on the bar before us. Behind him was a large mirror that reflected all three of us.

"That will be forty pounds," he said. I reached into my pocket, took out two Egyptian twenty-pound notes, and handed them over. The woman smiled, her white teeth sparkling in the mirror.

"Daniel," I said, clinking my beer bottle with hers.

"Maria."

"I'm glad to have met you, Maria. What are you doing in the bar?"

"I came to dance and to drink beer. My girlfriends are here, too."

She pointed to a table and the black women in miniskirts and high heels sitting beside it. They were drinking beer and watching the men at the billiard table. I'd seen a few of them here before, each always with a different man. They'd propositioned me, too, but I hadn't gone off with any of them.

This is a whore, I thought to myself, looking over the woman. *A whore just like the rest, who visits the bars at night. She's here for money.*

I took a big gulp of my beer. I wasn't particularly bothered by my realization. I'd returned lately from the Gaza Strip; I had money. I was already on the way to my fourth beer and was pleasantly drunk. I had nothing to do, and the sweltering Cairo summer had fired up my libido. Which is why I was hanging out in the Sudanese bars.

"I work for a foundation, actually," she added. "We deal with refugees."

"Well now, you can deal with me, too. I, for example, am a refugee."

"And just what are you fleeing?"

"Boredom."

She laughed and drank.

"What do you do?"

"Besides inviting beautiful women for beer?"

"Yes. Besides that."

"I'm a photographer."

"What do you take photos of?"

"People."

"What sort of people?"

"All sorts of people."

"Will you photograph me, too?"

"Maybe. It depends."

"On what?"

"Whether you're in trouble or not. I usually photograph people who are in trouble."

"Then I won't be your customer," she said with a laugh. "I'm not in trouble."

"Wait and see what happens," I said, downing my beer.

"But what trouble could I get into?"

"Well, you could fall hopelessly in love with me."

"That wouldn't be such big trouble."

"You don't know me."

"You have blue eyes."

"And on account of that you'll avoid trouble?"

"I like blue-eyed people. In South Sudan there are none."

"Is that where you grew up?"

"Yes."

"And will you return?"

"I don't think so. Cairo is a much better place than Jujuba."

The woman having finished her beer too, I waved to the bartender to bring us two more.

Soon the waiter put down the beers in front of us. I looked at my watch. It was 2 a.m.

"They're closing soon. How are you planning to spend the rest of the night?"

"It depends."

"On what?"

"On what you suggest."

"I have a bottle of vodka at home. If you're in the mood, you could come up to my place. We'll drink vodka and listen to music."

"Where do you live?"

"In Dokki."

"That's far."

"We'll go by taxi."

"Okay."

We left half the beer. I paid, and we then headed toward the exit. White cars were parked out in front of the bar, their drivers leaning up against their sides and smoking cigarettes while waiting for fares. They alone knew where the women were going, and they provided protection, too. They took customers around the city for ten times the normal rate. Maria talked at length in Arabic with one of the drivers, and after they came to terms we got into the Lada and headed off. We sat beside each other in the back seat. She smiled, and held my hand.

We kissed in the stairwell. My nose was filled with the fragrance of her skin. With a trembling hand I took my apartment keys from my pocket and opened the door.

"This is where you live?" she asked with a laugh on stepping inside and sizing up the room. The furnishings comprised only a bed and a table. My timeworn laptop lay on the table.

"Yes," I said, pulling her close and kissing her again. "Do you want vodka?"

"I do."

I went out to the kitchen, took the liquor from the fridge, and filled two glasses. By the time I returned, the woman had on only a bra on top.

"It's warm. I thought I'd take off my blouse."

"You thought right," I said, handing her the vodka.

"To those with blue eyes!" she said with a laugh. We clinked glasses, drank up, and set down the glasses beside the bed.

Her bra was black. Darker than her skin. Putting an arm around her waist, I kissed her again and unfastened the bra.

Her breasts were beautiful, with big, black nipples. She stepped out of her skirt. I, too, began getting undressed. A few seconds later I was already lying on top of her, kissing her face and neck. She moaned when I touched her and sighed, "Ay," when I closed my mouth around one of her nipples. I liked that a lot. I kept kissing her. I kissed the length of her belly and put my tongue into her navel. Her panties were black, too. With both hands I grabbed her ass, and then bore my face into her panties and pulled them off, too. My tongue moved down to her pubes but sought her clitoris in vain. Where it should have been, there was only an abnormal scar. Her vagina, too, was much smaller than what I was used to, and it was apparent where it had been sewn together.

I stopped, and for a couple of seconds stared, dumbfounded, at the scar.

"What is it?" asked the woman.

"A condom. I've got to go to the bathroom for a condom."

"Hurry," she said.

Standing up, and taking care so she wouldn't see my expression, I went to the bathroom and locked the door behind me. *Jesus Christ,* I thought, and stared at my face in the mirror. I saw before my eyes the mutilated cunt I was now supposed to stick my cock into. *I can do it,* I kept telling myself. *I just have to meanwhile imagine another cunt. That's all. I'm a pro at that.*

"Where are you already?" the girl called from the room.

"Just a moment," I said, removing the condom from the medicine cabinet and opening the bathroom door. I went not to the room but to the kitchen, for a swig of vodka. I took a great big gulp, and felt it go straight to my head.

"Is something wrong?"

"It took me a while to find it," I said, and stepped back into the room.

"I'll help you get it on."

She sat up on the bed, took my cock in her hands, and began playing with it. It took quite a few minutes of work with her hands and her mouth, too, before I managed to produce a modest erection. I pulled on the condom, whereupon she lay on her back and spread open her legs.

It was incredibly narrow. It hurt. Pressing my forehead against hers, I just kept moving, meanwhile watching her face.

"Ay," she moaned again and again, in a measured beat, and smiled. "Ay."

She can't have an orgasm, I thought to myself. I saw before me her being led into some tent in the middle of nowhere, being held down, and having her clitoris cut out with a razor blade. *It doesn't matter, anyway, the point is that I should come, since she's a whore.*

The thought that my cock was inside a mutilated cunt sapped all of my strength.

"What's wrong?" she asked when getting off me.

"Nothing."

"You haven't come," she said. "If you want," she added, caressing my chest, "I'll take you in my mouth."

"No, I don't want to."

"What's wrong?"

"Who did this to your cunt?" I asked.

"I was still a little girl. That's custom among them."

"You can't have an orgasm, right?"

"But it's really good."

"Can you have an orgasm?"

"Stop it already! Come on, kiss me and make love with me."

"You don't need to force it," I said.

I sat up in bed, reached down for my jeans, and took two hundred pounds out of it, which I pressed into her hand.

She stood and began dressing in silence. I didn't have a bit of strength; I could feel the liquor blurring my brain, and I was dizzy. *At least I paid her,* I thought while lying there on the bed. *I was a good customer.*

"I'm capable of being in love," she said with downcast eyes, already dressed. "Maybe I don't know things, like the women in your country, but I'm capable of being in love."

"That's good," I replied.

I heard the door close when she left.

Only in the morning did I notice that she'd left the money on the bed.

Banana Split

With the leftover beer I washed down two pills. I took Xanax to help me sleep. The first few weeks it worked, but as time passed, I had to take more and more. This evening I'd had two already, and now came two more.

Lying back in bed, I stared at the wall and waited for the effect. A half-hour passed, my eyes fixed on the mass of scribbles before me as I lay on the grimy sheet. "You're not alone," the previous tenant had written in letters of various sizes on every square centimeter of that wall. I got no sleepier or calmer. By 11 p.m. it was apparent that, yet again, I wouldn't get a wink of sleep. I stood up out of bed, reached for the phone, and called Blake. It rang.

"Where are you, you scoundrel?"

"In the Bussy Cat."

"Stay put."

In the sink I washed my face and underarms, got on a clean shirt, and set off. The receptionist, who was sitting in the lobby at a plastic table, watching soap operas on a 1970s color TV, turned his head toward me and said, "When will you pay? It is the end of the month."

He said it in English, with surprising precision, having presumably practiced the words to perfection. He'd had the opportunity, after all: the previous tenant had spoken English, too, until he killed himself.

"Soon," came my reply, in faultless Arabic, this being what I had practiced to perfection. My reply seemed not to phase him much: he turned his head back to the TV as I went on, down the steps and out to the street.

The Bussy Cat wasn't far from the Bluebird Hotel, where I lived. I had to walk two blocks. It was a fine example of a downtown bar where alcoholic Arabs imbibed. To get in you had to pass through a dark entryway that smelled of piss. Inside, too, it was dimly lit, the only source of light being the neon ads above the bar. Arabs were drinking away at the little tables. The filthy plastic tablecloths squelched each time they picked up their beers. Cigarette butts littered the floor along with the yellow shells of the chick peas served as finger food alongside the beer; the chick peas were salty and caused serious diarrhea. Everyone spit the shells on the floor.

Blake was sitting at the bar. Beside his right hand were four empty bottles of Stella.

"You look like shit," he said after I gave him a slap on the back and sat down beside him.

"You too."

"Thanks."

"My father died two days ago. What's your excuse?"

I ordered an Egyptian whiskey and downed it in one gulp. The turpentine flavor rushed down my spine.

"Got something? I know you do, you always do."

"I've got Xanax."

"That'll do. Xanax is good. It's funny to drink with. Let's have it." Taking the medication from my pocket, I pressed a few pills into his hand.

Greedily he snatched up a pill, swallowing it without even bothering to chew.

"Whiskey!" he shouted, bringing a fist down on the bar. The waiter produced a bottle of that same Egyptian whiskey, labeled "Ballantimes," with an *m,* poured a shot into his glass, and turned away.

"For him, too."

"I shouldn't. I already have two in me."

The waiter poured me another. Blake and I clinked glasses and drank up.

Blake asked for another round, and we drank that up too. "Got money on you?"

"Five hundred geneihs," I said, using the local term for Egyptian pounds.

"That's about as much as I have, too. Shall we head out to Ma'adi? I need a woman."

I looked at my phone: it was almost midnight. Even with a taxi, that leafy suburb was an hour south of downtown Cairo. It was too late for whoring. The Faris Bar closed at 2 a.m., and the prettier gals were taken by midnight.

"It's late already."

"No it isn't. It's never too late for drinking and whoring."

Blake put three hundred geneihs on the bar, asked and got the bottle of remaining whiskey in the bottle, and started toward the exit. I followed. In no time we found a taxi. By the time we reached the Nile, we'd finished the whiskey, and one more Xanax pill was in us each.

It was 1 a.m. by the time the taxi let us out in front of Faris. People were already trickling out.

"We're closing soon," said the bouncer, a black man, after giving us the once-over. Blake convinced him that we wanted only one drink and would then be on our way. He let us in.

There were barely a couple of people left inside. Before the bar was a mirror; I stared at myself. We were drunk but still moving. A thirtyish, long-legged Sudanese woman sat at the bar with a beer. She smiled on seeing us. Blake stepped over to her. "Hi, pretty girl."

"Hi."

"Are you alone? In need of company?"

"Yes," she said with a laugh.

Blake sat down beside her on a barstool, and I sat down beside them.

"This here is Daniel. I'm Charlie."

"Mira."

Blake kissed her hand.

"Mira. You're beautiful."

"You two are beautiful, too."

"So I am," said Blake. "Not the Hungarian."

"The Hungarian is beautiful, too. Are you American?"

"Yes. What are you drinking, Mira?"

"Beer."

Blake ordered three beers and three whiskeys.

We clinked the whiskey glasses and drank up.

"You remind me of an American singer, Mira," said Blake.

"Not Ella Fitzgerald, I hope."

"You know about Ella Fitzgerald?" I asked.

Mira nodded. "We used to listen to some of her records back in Khartoum."

"Beyonce," said Blake, putting an end to the guessing game.

We now clinked the beer mugs. The bartender warned us that this was the last round. Blake ordered three more whiskeys.

"Mira," he said, "both of us like you a lot, but this place is about to close. You'll have to choose between us."

"I can't choose."

"But you must."

"I live three blocks from here. You can both come over to my place for one more drink, so I can make a well-informed decision."

"You have booze at home?"

"No. But I have khat."

"We'll bring the booze," said Blake, telling the bartender to pack us up six cans of Sakar. The man put them on the counter in a black plastic bag. We paid.

Mira really did live just a couple of apartment buildings away. The wind blowing in from the desert sobered us up a helluva lot, Blake and I, by the time we reached her flat. It was in a two-story concrete block, like so many buildings in Ma'adi. The woman rummaged for a while in her golden purse until she found the key. Blake meanwhile pressed a hand to her ass, to which she said, with a laugh, "That's not allowed."

"Why not?"

"Because I haven't yet decided."

We entered a big living room that led to the other rooms and the bathroom. In the middle was a blue linen couch, a matching armchair right beside it, and a little table. Mira stepped from her high-heeled shoes and went in barefoot. We also took off our shoes. Blake put the black plastic bag on the table, removed a can of beer, opened it up, and plopped down in the armchair.

"Have you chewed khat before?" asked Mira with a grin.

"We have," I said.

"Good."

She went to the kitchen and returned with a plastic container. After peeling the lid off the box, she dipped in her finger and removed a big green glob of khat paste she then rubbed into her gums. We followed her example. I opened a beer to wash down the bitter taste.

Blake reached into his pocket and threw a leaf of Xanax pills on the table. Three pills were left.

"What is this?" asked Mira.

"Xanax," Blake replied. "It's terrific. Especially if you have a drink to go with it."

"What are the side-effects?"

Removing the flattened box from my pocket, I took out the information leaflet and read some of it aloud, choosing the most interesting bits.

"Consumption of alcohol is strongly ill-advised. Side effects may include agitation, irritability, anger, aggressive behavior, delusions, nightmares, hallucinations, psychosis, or other unusual behavior. If you experience any of these symptoms, contact your physician immediately."

"Aha," said Mira, swallowing a pill and laughing.

"So then," said Blake, "Have you decided already which one of us you like?"

Mira stood up and sat in Blake's lap. While kissing him she reached out a hand and began caressing my thigh.

"It's a really tough decision," she said with a laugh. "I like your mouth but the Hungarian's eyes. They are like broken glass."

Blake laughed.

"I've got to go to the bathroom," said Mira, "and when I come back I'll see how *he* kisses."

Extricating herself from Blake's embrace, she staggered toward the bathroom. By the time she returned, she was down to her bra on top, though she hadn't yet removed her skirt. She came straight to the couch, sat in my lap, and kissed me on the mouth. Her drool was bitter from the khat.

"I think you don't have to choose between us," said Blake, stepping up behind her and unfastening her bra.

I opened my eyes. The sun shone in the window, its light on the bed, where all three of us lay. I saw Blake's hairy leg beside mine, Mira's black nakedness between us. She was drooling onto the pillow. My mouth was dry, my lips cracked. My head was buzzing. Again I heard the noise.

"Mother."

A child's delicate voice came from the direction where, I suspected, the bedroom door was.

I shut my eyes.

"Mommy, wake up. Please wake up, Mommy, I have to go to school."

I lay there completely motionless. I dared not breathe.

"Mommy, I'm really hungry, too."

For a few seconds all was silent, and then I heard sniffling and crying from the door.

I turned to Mira and gave her a nudge.

"Wake up, your kid is calling you."

She didn't react. I nudged her harder. Her head slipped off the pillow. She didn't wake up.

The child didn't stop crying even for an instant. Sitting up in bed, I looked for my underwear. My head was buzzing, my temples throbbing. I felt as if a knife were being plunged into my head with every heartbeat. My underwear was under Mira, only its edge visible. I pulled it out and got it on fast. I then stepped over to the door, which was slightly ajar, and opened it completely. Standing by the bedroom was a little, dreadlocked black girl of about seven, wearing a floral dress and white shoes with ankle straps. Tears were flowing from her eyes.

"Hey, little girl," I said, my voice raspy from yesterday's whiskey and beer and Xanax.

"Where's my mommy?"

"Your mommy is asleep. She worked really late last night."

"Who are you?" she asked, sniffling, looking me over.

"I'm a friend of your mother's. My name is Daniel. Where is your father?"

"I don't know."

"Is there anyone besides your mother who helps out sometimes?"

"Miss Lucille. But she's not here now."

"I see," I said, massaging my throbbing temple.

"What's your name, little girl?"

"Ella."

"Okay, Ella. I'll get dressed and we'll find you something to eat."

Returning to the bedroom, I got on my jeans and T-shirt. I looked at the bed. Mira and Blake were lying there unconscious. The little girl was waiting for me in the living room, sitting, scared, on the couch. The khat paste and the empty cans of beer were still on the table along with the open condom-wrappers.

"Come on, Ella. Let's see if we find something in the kitchen."

She followed me there. Dirty dishes towered above the sink. I opened the old fridge. It was completely empty. For a minute I just stared at the sad little girl as I struggled with the nausea erupting within me.

"Today is a special day. We've met each other. Bring your things."

The little girl ran into one of the other rooms and reappeared a moment later with a cheap, Chinese knapsack on her back.

"Can we go?"

"We can go."

It was already hot outside. I kept blinking under the blazing sun, and my head hurt like hell.

"Where is your school?" I asked.

"Not far. At the end of the street."

We walked past two-story concrete apartment blocks that all looked the same, the plants in front of each building covered thickly with dust. At the corner I saw a sign for Costa Coffee, which had locations all over the place.

"We'll go in here for breakfast," I said.

The waiter raised his eyebrows on seeing me with a little girl, but said nothing. He stopped by our table.

"What do you want, Ella?" I asked.

"A banana split."

"I'd like a banana split and a coffee."

The waiter nodded, and left. I took a cigarette from my pocket and lit up.

"What would you like to be when you grow up, Ella?" I couldn't think of anything else to say.

"I want to be like Mommy. I want to make lots of money so we can buy a big house."

"I see. And where is your dad?"

"He stayed in Sudan."

"What does he do?"

"He's a soldier. Mommy says he died."

The waiter arrived, placing the dessert and the coffee on the table, and then left again. The banana split comprised two bananas, two scoops of vanilla ice cream, and chocolate sauce. The little girl wolfed it down at once.

"Once I'm grown-up and beautiful, like Mommy, I too will have nice clothes and white boyfriends. How did you meet Mommy?"

"In a restaurant," I replied.

"That's good. I like restaurants. Especially the desserts. Do you have a kid?"

"A little boy. He's still really little. He's not big, like you. He doesn't even talk yet."

"Is he white, too, like you?"

"Yes. And blond. Just like me."

"And is his mommy like mine?"

"Yes, just like yours."

I wiped her face with a napkin. She didn't like that at all. The waiter came by and I paid.

"Can you get to school on your own?" I asked her in front of the café.

"Of course. I'm a big girl."

"Bye, then."

Off hopped Ella along the street, turning around a couple of times to wave. Once she disappeared around the corner, I turned back toward Mira's building. I'd walked maybe a hundred meters when gut-wrenching nausea suddenly took hold of me. Leaning on a palm tree, I puked repeatedly. On finishing, I wiped off my mouth with the napkins that had been stuffed in my pocket and got to wondering when, the day before, I myself had eaten bananas.

When I got back to Mira's flat, there was Mira, naked, slumped on the couch. She clearly had a helluva hangover; pain was written all over her face.

"Don't worry about your kid. I bought her breakfast and took her to school."

For long seconds Mira just stared ahead with glassy eyes and cracked lips. I sat down beside her, in the armchair.

"I don't have a child," she said.

I took a big gulp of what was left of a can of beer. It was lukewarm, but it soothed my stomach.

The Most Beautiful Night of the Soul

"Don't you die, M'zungu," was Joyce's constant refrain. I think she meant it seriously, too. Why wouldn't a 300-pound Congolese madam mean such a thing seriously in the wee hours of the morning in Ma'adi, that leafy suburb of Cairo, during the last call for drinks at a dive bar or when the last customer leaves her place? The chair creaked under her as she leaned back, took a drag on her slender cigarette, took a swig of beer, and then she said it again, while resting her eyes upon me as if she saw death.

Of course it wasn't at all certain she was saying it to me. More likely she was saying it to her tribe back in the Democratic Republic of Congo, to orphaned child soldiers and witchdoctors left without followers. She was talking to someone from her past. In that respect we were different: I didn't go talking to my past. She did.

One time I asked her—after making love, having just wriggled my head out from between her colossal, swaying breasts, momentarily imagining that I'd just surfaced on the Mediterranean at night—why this never-ending mantra exhorting me not to die? As we lay there on her mattress, we watched the geckos racing across the ceiling of the prefab concrete apartment house and took labored breaths in the steaming hot Cairo night.

"Because it's custom."

Those in her tribe believe that on certain exceptional nights, under malicious stars, in the event of certain exceptional influences the soul leaves the body and sets forth on an expedition. They call this the "most beautiful night of the soul." At such times the soul is not bound by the sins of the flesh. But, left on its own, the body feels increasingly orphaned as it awaits the return of the soul, and if the soul doesn't return, the body dies. In Joyce's tribe it was custom to reassure the individual whose soul had wandered off not to die. They sat in front of their huts and on certain exceptional, starless nights they told each other, every single member of the tribe, not to die while his or her soul was away.

Of course souls don't leave everyone at the same time. To each his own time. But one thing's certain: no one can avoid having their soul abandon them sooner or later. At such times there's nothing to be done—besides being told by others not to die while your soul is away.

"Don't you die, M'zungu," said Joyce, adding my race in Swahili. "Don't you die, white boy!"

I never did understand why she was saying it to me, of all people. Why not to her workers? Her customers? Why not anyone else? When I asked her, she replied that it's because she saw that my soul happened to be off somewhere.

Perhaps she really did believe in the spell, I thought, or perhaps she was just being sentimental or was crazy, until one day I found in her room the letter notifying her, with regrets, that her son had died in Congo in a battle against the rebels.

So it was in vain that she escaped with the kid after her village was massacred. It was in vain that she left him with her sister in the capital, so that by going from the peaceful and tolerant Sudan to that city of opportunity, Cairo, she could earn enough money to have them join her. Her efforts were wasted. The fact that someone is just six years old protects them from nothing at all in most of Black Africa.

The postmark on the letter was from the day she first raised me up off the street.

"Don't you die, M'zungu," she said when we first met. It was Wednesday, 2 a.m. A hot wind was blowing in from the desert in this suburb of Cairo. Filthy palm trees stood in the light of the yellow moon. I was bleeding heavily.

It had begun as a wondrous night, actually: just me and the liquor. It began with me packing my things into my backpack and checking out of the Bluebird Hotel. I didn't have enough money left to pay for the room. I had not the slightest intention of getting in touch with Europe, from where I could have arranged to get myself some money. I simply figured that nothing mattered. I didn't really care what would happen, but I was certain that I could spend what I had left on better things than the cockroach-infested room I'd been renting for three months, and in which the ghost of the previous tenant had still been merrily haunting me, that fellow who'd committed suicide while lying in bed. After taking my leave of the blood-stained mattress and the walls scribbled over with ink, I headed toward Ma'adi, on the city outskirts, where the rocky desert begins. After a brief search, I found the Koriana brothel.

Cairo's suburbs are full of whores. Mainly black Africans. The products of war and poverty, they flee to Egypt, which, in contrast with Europe, is more accessible. Of course not a single one of these hapless women arrives in the country as a prostitute, but becomes one subsequently. When they realize that they can earn far more money from letting strangers between their legs than they can from cleaning or working as maids. They won't be any more scorned than they already are: it was the Arabs, after all, who conquered her ancestors and then sold them into slavery. And while that practice has since gone mostly out of fashion, the vast majority of the population does not regard black people as their equals, no matter how much money they have or what they do for a living.

Though I'd already been to nearly all the brothels in Cairo, I never had figured out how their owners named them. In the Koriana, which means "Korean" in Arabic, I never did see a single Korean. As for the Faris, it had originally been a Chinese restaurant, and though the name "Red Dragon" did change under the new owner, the furnishings in the lobby did not. The dragon-themed folding screens and the plastic tablecloths with Chinese characters remained. It was here that the businesswomen sold their bodies, and here that so many of the city's black African residents imbibed.

When I stepped inside the Koriana, only a couple of people were sitting about in front of the mirrors, and the only billiard table was occupied. Two black guys and two black girls were playing. Judging from their facial features, they were all Sudanese.

I sat down at the bar and ordered a beer and a whiskey. An Arab woman in her mid-twenties put the drinks down before me. I sipped on the whiskey and glanced about. Though I didn't have a whole lot of money left, it was by all means enough for one woman. Enough, too, so I could drink late into the night. I didn't care about the rest. More precisely, for ninety-two days now I hadn't cared where I would sleep and what I would eat, who would pay the electric bill, and who would shoo away the residents' representative when he came knocking. I didn't care how many people had died in the protests and how many in the bombings in Gaza, I didn't care about the spokespersons campaigning for the true causes set to change the world, and I didn't care about the sad-faced dogs and even sadder-faced subjective poets whose images were shared on Facebook. I'd had enough of everything.

Like I said: It was a wondrous evening, just me and the liquor.

As time passed, more and more people filtered into the bar, and finally even moving was impossible. To be on the safe side I downed three more whiskeys. Once I finally felt as if the alcohol had smoothed over my face, I went looking for a woman. Choice, there was. At a table behind me sat five black women bearing gobs of makeup and seriously gelled hair and wearing cocktail dresses. They were whores, around thirty years old; they were looking about and drinking beer. One of them, a rather thin girl in a tight-fitting white dress, stood up and stepped over to me.

"Hello there. Are you alone?"

"Not anymore. What's your name?"

"Pocahontas."

"I didn't even know there are American Indians in Sudan."

"You can't know everything."

She laughed, and sat down on the barstool beside me.

I hadn't batted an eyelid when she'd said her name moments earlier. In the months prior I'd heard dozens of fanciful names, from Mona Lisa to Madonna. The girls would say anything they thought the men would find exciting, anything at all that was suitable to mask the huts they'd come from, without running water or electricity, and the witchcraft-inspired names they'd gotten from their mothers. All the shady bars and brothels were full of Madonnas, Mona Lisas, and Pocahontases.

"Will you have something to drink?" I asked, unable to resist staring at her breasts. They were small, with pugnacious, big nipples.

"Beer."

I waved at the waitress, who brought out the drinks. We drank.

"I'd like to spend the whole night with you," I said.

Pocahontas laughed, her eyes glistening.

"You'll have to pay for that. Five hundred geneihs. I'm a businesswoman."

"I'm not American. I don't have money. I have two hundred geneihs altogether."

"Two hundred fifty."

"Two hundred."

"I'll think about it."

From the way she'd said it, I knew we'd settled on the price. I turned to the bar to order another round of drinks. That's when the problems began.

A paunchy, fifty-something Brit appeared from out of thin air and stepped between me and the girl. I knew the type. He was with the British Embassy and didn't work a bit, and yet every month he took home double what I make from wars. He started talking to Pocahontas.

"Sorry," I said, and tried sitting back on my seat.

"Beat it," the bloke replied in a gurgling voice.

That's all I needed. I gave him a right hook. He was on the floor at once.

I should not have hit him.

The British Embassy staff go whoring about together. Three characters the size of small trucks came charging at me immediately, SAS tattoos on their arms. They must have been the embassy's gardener, pastry chef, and shoeshine boy, since officially not a single foreign mission was allowed to have its own soldiers in Egypt.

The first drove a fist twice into my face. The first blow cracked my nose, the next one tore the skin at my eyebrows. I was already on the ground.

The others joined in only once I'd fallen. Their fists rained down on my head, they kicked me, and once I was no longer moving and not even trying to defend myself, they dragged me out in front of the bar and flung me onto the street. My backpack came flying after me in a big arch from the door, and I heard my laptop's monitor implode as it hit the ground. The bouncers looked on the whole scene with stoic calm, and when the gardener, pastry chef, and shoeshine boy went back inside the bar, the bouncers pulled me a bit to the side, by some bushes, so I wouldn't disturb the flow of business with my bleeding.

Just how long I lay there on my back among the bushes, choking and half-blind from my own blood, I have no idea.

I felt a boundless calm. I watched the stars in the sky, the flickering lights of the many quasars and galaxies, and I kept thinking that this was exactly the distance I was from what people call a meaningful life. My brooding was interrupted by a deep, woman's voice.

"Don't you die, M'zungu," said Joyce and lifted me up off the ground. We knew each other in passing from the Faris. Late one night we'd had a beer.

"Don't you die, M'zungu," she said while helping me into her rented house on the edge of the desert, and as she then sat me down on the edge of her bed and untied my boots.

"Don't you die," she said as she wet a towel and, with a well-practiced hand, washed the blood out of my eyes.

"M'zungu," she whispered as she took off her clothes and lay down beside me.

"There is no death."

Her two colossal breasts covered me from the world as surely as a total eclipse of the moon.

Making love with a prodigious black woman is unlike anything you've ever experienced if you are fair-skinned and from a land where this is unlikely to have been part of your reality. The oscillating mass, whose every last feature was far from what I'd learned to perceive as beautiful, was mesmerizing. If you were once a provider, a father, a husband, and are then no longer these things, you can only define yourself by what you are not. If such traditional structures have betrayed you, if you no longer give a shit about them, and if you happen to be in the right part of the world, having come from elsewhere—then you sleep with women only because that's what the scorching heat that has penetrated your bones dictates. Bathing in sweat, your heart hammering away, all you can think of is that you must make love or die. You take serious measures to ensure either option.

Joyce was different than any woman I'd ever encountered as a man. Her beautiful body, more than 300 pounds, nearly pressed the life out of me when she lay upon me. Her sweat smelled of spices.

Many black Africans regard white people's sweat as among the most intolerable smells of all. Our sweat is vinegary, so they say, and, in contrast with that of Arabs or blacks, it stinks from afar. There may be something to this. Everyone in the house smelled good, though they sweated just the same as I did.

For three days straight I didn't even get up out of Joyce's bed. Figuring mightily into this was the fact that the Brits had given me a rather sound beating. I was blue and green everywhere, and breathing came hard.

She lived in a two-story concrete house. Her room had one window, with a worn, black wooden frame. That window afforded a good view of the desert access road. When Joyce went down to the kitchen, or for some reason left me alone, I'd stare at length out at the aged Lada station-wagons rolling along toward the Sinai Peninsula. The wind would catch the scarves of the barefoot Bedouin drivers, and those scarves would then flutter outside of the rolled-down windows.

We lay on a two-person old colonial-era bed that creaked at our every move. Opposite the bed was a closet with a mirror, and beside that, a makeup table. For three days straight even she hardly left the room. We made love, or else, in the unbearable heat, we ate opium. We didn't talk much.

The third night, after we had the falafel sandwiches Joyce brought for supper, I stood up and began getting dressed.

"Where are you going?" she asked.

She sat up in bed, her huge breasts swinging forward like two waterskins, the sweat glistening on her body.

"I don't know. Away."

"Why?"

"Because I've overstayed my welcome to begin with. I'm sure you're bored of me."

"I'm not bored of you, M'zungu. Where are you going?"

"Why should you care? I'm no one to you."

"You sleep with me."

"I sleep with anyone."

"Do you have a place to go?"

"Not yet, but I will. That never was a problem before."

"Where will you sleep?"

"In some hotel."

"Stay."

"Why do you want me to stay?"

"Because you sleep with me, and beyond that, it could only help the business if there's a man here."

I lit a cigarette and thought to myself that it didn't matter at all.

"What would my duties be?"

"To watch over the girls."

"I can't even watch over myself."

"It's enough if you're seen."

"Okay."

"Hey, come on," she said, and led me down to the kitchen.

The kitchen was on the ground floor by the girls' rooms, opposite the massive front door. A large space that smelled of grease with a charmless wooden table and plastic chairs in the middle. Its two windows looked out onto the yard, affording a view of sickly palm trees with filthy leaves and garden plants faded to the color of sand. No one took care of the yard.

The kitchen was the heart of the house, with its eight-holed greasy black gas-stove. This is where the young women who lived in the house gathered every night; it was here that they spoke of their days, their customers, and it was here that they paid Joyce her due for the lodging, their visas having been arranged, their new lives in Cairo. They were loud. Their laughter and squealing filled the house every night. They were the faithful companions of my never-ending insomnia, for until the sun didn't rise in all its full light, there was always someone there to talk to.

Joyce employed four women. Not one was older than thirty. The oldest among them was called Mina, and she, like Joyce, had come from the Belgian Congo. The other girls were South Sudanese, from Juba or environs. Samiya and Brinda were sisters, with serious ideas about and plans for life; and little Yaya, who couldn't have been a day older than eighteen, regularly sent money to her family back home.

It was well after midnight the first time Joyce led me down to the kitchen. All four young women were sitting around the table. Their makeup had already smeared, and they were in panties and T-shirts. They were smoking and drinking cheap, Egyptian beer. Each one of them fell silent when we stepped in.

"Who is this?" asked Mina, breaking the silence and provocatively placing her foot up on the table. Her eyes burned with hatred.

"This is M'zungu, my friend," said Joyce. "He'll be staying here for a bit."

"It's bad luck to let a white man stay for long in a house."

"This is my house."

"It still brings bad luck."

The other girls snickered, and gazed at me with curiosity.

"This one doesn't bring bad luck."

"How do you know?"

"I know, and that's that. I didn't ask for your opinion. If you don't like something here, you can leave."

Mina turned her eyes down and took a gulp of her beer."

"As you want, Big Mama. Keep your M'zungu. But don't forget I warned you."

"I think he's got a really sweet face," said Brinda, laughing along with her sister. Yaya then spoke, noting that the worst customers were those men who first went cheating on their wives before coming here, since a girl needed to work on them forever before they were able to produce a respectable erection.

Joyce took two beers from the fridge, pressed one into my hand, and sat down in an empty chair.

"How many were there today?" she asked the young women. They then began haggling loudly over the money.

I was Joyce's lover.

During the day I alone was awake. The women, who invariably went to sleep toward dawn, rarely awoke before noon, and it almost never happened that they'd emerge from their rooms until the air didn't cool down enough to be tolerable.

Life in the house began at 5 p.m. Until then I occupied myself as best I could. I did the necessary shopping and I sat in front of a white sheet of paper onto which—such was my conviction—I should write something, or else I lay back down beside Joyce and watched her measured, heavy breathing.

In European terms, Joyce's house would not have qualified as a brothel. Men never arrived on their own, and it wasn't advertised anywhere. The women working for Joyce were the living advertisements of the service provided, the sales reps, and the transactors in one. Joyce only provided the rooms and made it possible for them to live legally in Egypt. For that, she paid lots of money to officials at the immigration agency.

When those in the house began waking up in the late afternoon, at first all I could hear were the toilets being used, and then the radios were turned on in the rooms and Egyptian pop music began blaring. The cacophony didn't bother anyone. The women ran about the house half-naked, brushed their thick black hair in front of the mirrors or shouted at each other if one of them occupied the bathroom for too long.

They quarreled, and then they made peace in a flash. The fights came easily to blows. If one girl got on another's clothes or used up another's perfume or hairspray, the owner unhesitatingly fell at her, yanking away at her hair and wrestling with her on the floor with such vehemence that the others had to intervene. And yet such brawls petered out just as fast as they erupted. The women, who minutes before had been at each other with unbounded hostility, were now sitting beside each other, laughing, having what to them was breakfast, like inseparable friends.

Preparations took until 9 p.m.—all the way until Joyce gave the command to begin. The girls would have been capable of spending all night primping themselves, straightening their hair with flat irons and then spraying or gelling or waxing their hair rock-hard, if Joyce didn't roar at them that it was time for the night to begin. When we stepped out the door, the company looked as if headed for the opera, each woman in her cocktail outfit, with black pantyhose and high-heel shoes.

They divvied up their hunting grounds among the African bars in Ma'adi. Two girls always went to the Faris and two to the Koriana or else to some ship docked on the Nile. Their first order of business was to catch Western men for themselves, for such men were both the gentlest and paid the most. The Arabs were wilder, with less cash to spare, but if there were no other takers, the women went with them, too, as well as with visitors from relatively affluent black African countries.

There were regulars, too. Awaiting the women in the bars were diplomats from abroad and staff at international NGOs—men who by day fought fiercely for human rights and issued proclamations left and right condemning prostitution, only so that at night, woozy from cheap Egyptian alcohol, they could then work off their built-up stress with the girls.

The price of the service varied by the customer, but the women didn't go with anyone for under two hundred Egyptian pounds, or geneihs. When they made a deal, they sent Joyce a text message letting her know they were headed off. At such times we too left the bar, where we'd been drinking, and the girls made sure that Joyce would always get home first.

I think it was the occasion on which I involuntarily became an active participant in the business that the girls accepted that I, too, was a bona fide resident of the house.

One evening toward midnight Joyce and I were drinking between the dragon-ornamented folding screens of the Faris when someone began roaring my name. I turned toward the sound. Sitting in a corner with three other men was a New York City guy I knew from the local English-language paper. He was a well-heeled Jewish kid from Brooklyn whose sense of mission and need to prove himself had swept him all the way to Cairo, where he was learning Arabic. He was now sitting about with group of men who, while varied, all looked American.

"Hey, Daniel, what's up, you old warrior?" he said. "Come have a drink with us."

I headed toward them and tried remembering his name. It came to me.

"David. It's been a while. What's up?"

"A whiskey for my friend!" David shouted to the bar.

The waitress brought the whiskey. We clinked glasses and drank.

"You're still traveling about in wars?" he asked me.

"Yes."

"This kid is crazy, I tell you," David said to his friends. "But he's charged his way through the Egyptian and Libyan revolutions. And how many times have you been to the Gaza Strip?"

"Fourteen."

"Fourteen? Like I said, this kid is crazy!"

"What are you guys doing here?" I asked. "I've never seen you in this bar."

"We got a tip that there are girls here. You know, men need to satisfy certain needs of theirs. Do you think those two women there at the bar are whores?"

I turned to look. Two girls were sitting at the bar, but neither worked for Joyce.

"I don't know. Maybe. If I was in your shoes I'd be careful. It's easy to pick up something you don't want to."

"You're right, Daniel. But where in Cairo can we find clean working women, where?"

We went on drinking, and I looked over those at the table. They were young, middle-class men in their early twenties. They were exuberant on account of the booze.

"But you can."

"Where?"

"I know a phone number. But I'm sure they're not cheap."

"Call them over here right away."

I stood from the table and stepped over to Joyce.

"One hundred fifty dollars apiece," she said.

I sauntered back to the guys' table and told them the price.

"That's nothing," came the reply, and they ordered more drinks.

A half-hour later the four girls arrived from the house and took home the four men. They later reported that they were shy, bashful kids without any sexual experience. They posed no problems. They paid like troopers, and one or two even returned almost every week. Given that one hundred fifty dollars was almost as much as they made all week, the girls were enormously satisfied with me. Mina now even overlooked the fact that I was white. From then on I always had to look around the bars to see if I might happen upon an acquaintance to whom I could recommend our services.

It almost never happened that anyone spent the whole night at the house. After orgasm, most customers, overcome by shame, left the premises as quickly as possible. By no later than 4 a.m. the house emptied out entirely, and the girls gathered in the kitchen to talk over their day and give Joyce her due, a third of their proceeds.

Joyce showed no mercy in collecting the sums. She never let anyone go to sleep until she was paid. She bound the takings with a hair tie. The thick, filthy wad of cash was always on her. She slept that way, too, with the money in her hand, or else she placed it beside her face, on the pillow, close enough so she could smell it.

"Why do you sleep with the money?" I asked her late one night as we prepared for bed.

"Because, unlike people, money doesn't die, that's for sure; it doesn't flee, and you don't need to raise it. You can place your unconditional trust in money."

"Don't you die, Joyce," I said after an extended silence.

"I won't die, M'zungu, don't you worry about me, I'm fine. But things are not all in order with you."

"There's nothing wrong with me."

"But there is."

"What?"

"You speak to ghosts during the night."

"That's not such a big problem."

"You speak to ghosts even when you're awake."

Not for a moment was Joyce jealous of the other women living in the house. Only once did she say, "Today you desired a thin girl." We'd been laying beside each other in her bed, looking at the geckos emerging from the cracks in the wall, while I, drunk on Egyptian rum, didn't have it in me to make love to her.

That day I did fuck Brinda. How Joyce got wind of it, I have no idea, but she knew. At the same time, she didn't ascribe much importance to it. Joyce didn't live in a shell: she knew precisely that, in and of itself, to go to bed with someone does not necessarily mean more than a momentary expression of mutual affinity. I had some sort of personal relationship with each of the women during the month I spent in the house. Not once did it happen, though, that I didn't return to Joyce's side. I slept every night through beside her.

Brinda and Samiya were the first. It was Sunday, the first regular workday of the week, and as such, a rather unbusy day for the girls. There wasn't much traffic in the bars, which closed earlier, in fact, than on other days of the week. At such times the girls went off into the city to take care of their personal matters. Joyce went, too, to pay allotments to the various bureaucrats who decided which among the Africans could get a visa to stay in Egypt and who couldn't. So too, she would pay the police chief of the Ma'adi district, who, among other things, was responsible for ensuring local morals in the suburbs. I did not accompany her on these errands of hers. She was concerned, after all, that the prices would go up if the officials saw that she was with a white man.

This fear of hers was completely justified.

In Africa and the poor countries of the Middle East, everyone imagines that white folks have money even under their skins. Aside from the obvious disadvantages, this also means that regardless of just how you look and what condition you're in, you'll be let in anywhere in the hope of getting money out of you. If this happens in error, by the time that gets out, it's way too late to do anything about it.

It was Sunday. I was alone in the house with Brinda and Samiya in the afternoon heat. I was sitting in the kitchen drinking a beer when Brinda ran in. She had on a bra and panties.

"Come with me," she said.

She led me into her room, where the TV was on.

"Is it true that doctors are free in Europe?"

"Where did you hear that?"

"They said it on TV."

"Yes, in a few countries. You have to pay a general fee, which isn't too much. Not that the service is all that good."

"It must be better than in Juba."

"Yes, probably."

She fell silent for a bit, pondering what I'd said.

"And where you're from, snow falls?"

"Yes. In winter."

"And is it very cold?"

"Yes."

"Not hot as hell, like in Africa."

Reaching back with her hands, she unfastened her bra.

"Don't you think my breasts are too small?"

"No," I said, and heard my blood beating in the back of my neck. Her breasts were perfect, with pointy little nipples.

"Well, I think they are. If I have the money, I'll have them fixed."

"You don't need to do a thing with your breasts."

"Touch them. You'll feel how small they are."

I touched them, and in the same motion we plunged right into bed.

After we finished, I lit a cigarette. She took it from my hand, took a drag, and gave it back.

"I knew you're special from the moment I first saw you in the house," she said.

"Really?"

"It was love at first sight. Yes. I knew I'd be your wife, and we'd live together in Europe."

"Are you really in love with me?"

"Yes. Very."

"And do you know my name?"

"M'zungu."

"My proper name."

She fell silent. I stood up out of bed and began getting dressed.

"Really, I love you very much," she said as I left the room.

In what remained of the afternoon she listened to sad, Arabic love songs in her room, but by evening she seemed as good as new. She sat there in the kitchen laughing along with the others, with only a few reproachful glances revealing just how offended she was. I felt bad for a few days on account of what had happened, but then one night she had a white customer she herself had found in the Faris. So her performance would come off as more credible, she didn't even ask him for money.

Though I was completely certain that she had let in everyone on our fleeting romance, that didn't stop her sister, Samiya, from trying something similar on me a few days later. They hated Africa with all their hearts.

Yaya was a thin, tall girl with an alarmed look in her eyes. She was the youngest in the house. She had that air of innocence which, after thirty, leaves a person without a trace. With childlike sincerity she was able to be happy about anything, even about anyone else's happiness. Though it wasn't said aloud, all of the other women treated her like a child, guarding her: they didn't let the wilder customers lay their hands on her, nor did they let her drink as much as they themselves drank. I asked Joyce how Yaya had ended up in the house.

Yaya was from the Zaghawa tribe in Darfur. As a young child she'd wound up in Khartoum in the course of a UN rescue mission, and from there, with the support of an Egyptian American foundation, to the foundation's orphanage school in Egypt. Unfortunately, however, as international media attention on Darfur waned, so too did the monies flowing into the foundation, which finally couldn't pay its bills and had to close. Children under twelve were lucky, since finding them adoptive parents overseas was easy. Yaya, however, was past twelve, and so along with several of her peers, no one needed her.

Of course the foundation paid some money to the state child welfare office for her use and to track the girl's fate, but in chronically overpopulated Egypt, where many thousands of Egyptian children live on the streets, the sums transferred to Yaya vanished in the system without a trace. Soon she was on the streets. Just how long she lived the life of an Egyptian street kid was anyone's guess, but one day a madam by the name of Lina discovered her and gave her work. Joyce had inherited Yaya from her along with the house. That had been five years earlier, when Lina had to leave the country in a flash at the order of the immigration authorities. I never did figure out exactly why Lina had been deported. But that it was back to Sudan, that much was clear; for Yaya sent her money to Juba weekly, right on schedule. In African terms, substantial sums. She must have done so because Lina was the closest thing she had to family.

I'd been living in the house for several weeks when, one day, Yaya posed her question. She approached me in the early morning hours in the kitchen. She was in street clothes, without makeup. She sat down beside me on one of the chairs. She pulled a wad of wrinkled hundred-geneih notes from her red wallet, smoothed them out with care, and placed them before me on the table.

"Daniel, I'd like to ask you for something.'

"What would that be?"

"Could you send this money for me to Juba? I have to go to the government office building, the Mogamma, for my passport."

"Sure. With Western Union?"

I knew that the bureaucratic procedure ahead of her that day would take at least twelve hours, that she wouldn't have time for anything else at all. Alongside the pyramids and the ancient ruins, the Mogamma, on Tahrir Square, is Egypt's biggest architectural attraction. From the 1950s on, anyone who wanted any sort of official permit had to get it in the Mogamma. The building did not grow with the population, however. It is a maze of hallways, some leading who knows where and others coming to dead ends, stacked high with typewritten files and full of cafés and so many secretive windows serving some inscrutable function, behind which, year by year, some ninety million citizens are registered, issued numbers, and have their documents stamped.

Expedited service took twelve hours. That meant you managed to bribe someone who knew precisely which window you had to stand in line at with your request. A whole industry had grown up in the Mogamma to accommodate even this service.

Every foreigner also had to visit the Mogamma, for that was where visas were issued, too. Of course, as a Westerner I enjoyed advantages. In contrast with those from Africa, I didn't have to go in every three months to renew my residence permit. Only once a year. It was in the course of one such visit that I saw a family make a tiny fire in a hallway, and while the head of the household cooked supper, the mother nursed the three little kids in her arms.

"Yes," said Yaya. "with Western Union. Send the money to Lina Oruba in Juba. Send me the transfer code."

"Got it."

"Thank you," she said with a sigh and left the kitchen. For a while I just stared at the banknotes lying on the table before me. Then I got dressed and went into the city. The only Western Union office money could be sent from was downtown. It was already full of people by the time I arrived, mainly those from the city's black African community waiting to send money home. I waited two hours for my turn. On finishing, I texted the code to Yaya. Then I sat about in a downtown café with wood chips all over its floor. Finally I went back to the house.

Yaya returned in the late afternoon. The girls were already well underway preparing for the night.

"Come with me," she said.

She led me to her room. As soon as I stepped in, she closed the door behind me. She began undressing. First she removed her T-shirt, and then her pants. She stood before me completely naked. She was beautiful and very young.

"Just what are you doing?" I asked.

"I want to thank you for taking care of the Western Union transfer for me. Come on."

"You don't have to thank me," I said.

Mina hated whites with all her heart. She declared this whenever the opportunity arose. True, that didn't keep her from lying down with white customers, too. To her mind, whites spread communicable diseases and stank, always had underhanded motives, and were bent on ravaging proper folks. She hated me from the moment I moved in. She kept reminding me by way of pointed observations, usually in front of everyone who lived in the house. Once, for example, she explained at length that when with men of my sort it's best to pull not just one but two condoms on them. For one thing, because then it was certain they wouldn't infect a girl with a thing, and, moreover, because then there would be no child even if the man were to deliberately rip the outside condom. Men of my sort were out to get decent girls pregnant, after all.

I didn't really bother with her. I had my own issues. I kept my distance from her, and after a while she stopped hounding me and making such remarks. But distilled hatred still always radiated from her eyes. Or, well, almost always. She had a longtime Egyptian customer. A fat, mustachioed dentist. He must have weighed as much as Joyce. But that's not what made him special.

"His prick is gigantic," said Mina, extending her hands about twelve inches apart. Since he was a weekly regular who paid respectably, she always managed an orgasm—but the act hurt her every time. It was in vain that she prepared herself both physically, with various creams, and emotionally. The result was always the same. She felt as if she'd been kneaded and ripped apart. And that's just how she looked. After finishing with the man, she sat for hours in the kitchen with her knees up to her chin and stared straight ahead. One night, when I got home a bit sooner than the others, that's how I found her.

"Are you okay?" I asked, but she didn't reply.

Slowly, one motion at a time, she got up off the chair, put her weight on a foot, and started out of the kitchen. Would have started, that is: after two steps toward the door, she collapsed. She would have hit the floor, had I not caught her. I took her in my arms and into her room, and lay her down on the bed. Blood was flowing from her.

"Stay here," she said.

I stayed. She pressed her head to my chest.

In the morning, when she awoke, she gave me a flustered look.

"May I ask you something?" I said while getting up from the bed.

She nodded.

"Why do you hate white people?"

"I don't hate white people."

"No?"

"No. How could I hate my own daughter?"

Once she regained her strength, she again hated me with all her heart.

I'd already been living at Joyce's for three weeks when madness entered my life. Literally. My move there had ensured me a bit of a routine, true, but insomnia still held my head in its grips, even if I was at least leading a sexual life of sorts with some regularity and I was surrounded by respectable, working people.

Those respectable, working people usually slept through the morning. I was already awake by the time the muezzins called the faithful to the Fajr prayer, and with bloodshot eyes I gazed out at the sun rising over the desert, opened a can of beer, or put on the coffee. I liked it when there was silence in the house; for hours I'd just sit there, looking out of my head. All was perfect.

I'd already been undergoing my daily meditation in this manner for three weeks when, one morning, madness stepped into the kitchen. It was blond, blue-eyed, two years old. It didn't greet me, but just sat down beside me on a chair and simpered at me. It didn't have to say a thing. I knew the bell tolled for me.

With suspicion I watched my son, who, I knew beyond a doubt, could not be here, since he was 3,500 kilometers away, with his mother. Just to be sure, I flung my mug of coffee at him. With nimbleness that defied his age, he ducked.

"Where is your mother?" I asked.

He didn't answer.

"What do you want?"

Silence. He just sat there, swinging his legs.

I broke out in a cold sweat. I stood, picked the pieces of the mug up off the floor, and wiped away the spilled coffee. I sincerely hoped that by clutching onto the last bit of information about reality that had crossed my mind—that I had no idea where my child was just now, but that there was no way he could be here—my hallucination would soon pass.

I hoped that, as had always been the case, the vision would last only a few minutes and then fade away, allowing me to return to what I'd been doing just before. But now the kid was breathing down my neck all day. Most unnerving of all was that, in keeping with his two years of age, he didn't talk a whole lot. He mostly just stood there, simpered, and stared. The others didn't see him and didn't even hear him stir, so I tried pretending he wasn't there. This worked for a while. Until I lost my patience and my cool. Now, Kristóf really didn't say much, but when he did speak, it was terribly irritating, for he went on and on about how I should behave. All my life I'd been quick to jump whenever someone told me what to do and how to do it, and I sure hadn't expected this of my own child. Especially since I knew he was just a ghost.

The women and I were sitting in the kitchen celebrating when he first told me off. Yaya had gotten her residence permit extended at the Mogamma by another year. They'd bought two crates of Stella light beer and three bottles of "Ballantimes" Egyptian whiskey—yes, with an "m"—for the occasion. We began drinking when the last customer left the house. The women were drinking respectably, and it was all I could do to keep up with them. They drank on account of anything. The sweltering heat that quivered between the walls of this concrete house; Africa, which they'd brought with them but that they missed; for the end of the day; and this unbearably shitty work of theirs.

I'd just opened my fourth can of beer when the kid spoke. I'd already completely forgotten that he was there.

"Don't drink a lot," he said in my mother tongue.

He cast a worried look.

"Fuck you," I replied, and drank up the beer in my hand in one go.

"Don't drink a lot."

"What does it matter, after all?"

"Don't drink a lot."

"I'll do what I want."

The women didn't say a thing. In silence they watched my chitchat with the kitchen corner. When I realized what was happening, to save the situation, I opened another can of beer.

"There's nothing better than a can of cold beer at the end of the day," I said.

After the kitchen incident I was especially on guard not to reveal myself to anyone. *There's nothing wrong with being mad as long as it's not obvious to others*, I thought. This worked, too. Not that that stopped the kid from butting into my life again and again. For example, he was sitting there in the Faris when I punched a drunk American asshole named Dennis. He'd begun shoving and groping the girls, calling them whores to their faces. Though his assertions were true, I hit him all the same. It's one thing, what line of work you're in. Who can call it by its name, is another thing. My fist landed right on his nose and he went flying across the room, slamming against the wall of the bar. I was truly surprised at how much I'd enjoyed it. I had hit not only the dumb American but everything I had a problem with. Hungary got a blow, as did my child's mother and her family, all those rotten scumbags who blustered on and on about morals. Blood flowed from the American's nose as he sat hunched up on the floor, protecting his face with a hand. I would have gone after him to hit him a bit more, but the kid, who until then had been passively observing the incident, all at once stepped right between me and the downed American.

"Don't," he said, taking my hand.

"Don't *what?*" I shouted, tearing my hand from his and running out of the bar.

Of course I finally learned to ignore him completely. But this didn't irritate him in the least. His comments made me really furious, but aside from Joyce I didn't speak with anyone about it.

I broached the subject one Sunday night. Joyce and I were sitting in the Koriana drinking Cubanas. Our mood wasn't good. The khamsin was raging outside. The red-hot wind snatched up the sand in the desert and showered it upon the city, where you could hardly get a breath and couldn't see a thing. The streets turned into walls of sand. The khamsin is always hellish in Cairo. Right up next to the desert, it is intolerable.

Our mood wasn't good. The May sandstorm had a vice grip on everyone's heads, pressing them down toward the ground. It was hard to resist even in closed, air-conditioned spaces.

It was past eleven when Joyce met up with an old acquaintance of hers. A black woman in her mid-thirties. Gold-colored hoop earrings shone on the side of her head. Her name was Stella, she was from Mombasa, and big scabs crisscrossed her face. We sat there politely drinking the beer. I joked that her name was the same as the Egyptian light beer when Joyce wiped her brow and said she was going home, but that we should stay if we felt like it. I stayed.

Stella, who happened to have money on her, ordered another Cubana. When we finished half the bottle, she said I was handsome and asked if I wanted to go up to her place, which was nearby. Since Joyce had caught the last taxi stationed in front of the bar, I figured anything was better than walking nine blocks through the raging sandstorm.

Stella really did live nearby, in a one-room hole in the wall. She explained that it was pretty messy. Her bed was a filthy mattress. We fell upon each other at once to minimize the pressure. Then the woman excused herself, saying she had to use the bathroom. I began peeling my pants off myself when I saw my kid.

"Get on a rubber," he said.

I stared at him in silence.

"Get on a rubber," he repeated.

"Okay," I replied.

I didn't have a condom with me, so I began looking for one in the room. Nothing. On one of the little tables, though, I found a bunch of used syringes and a bag full of brown heroin. It was right there in front of me. How could I have missed it on stepping into the flat? I got my pants and T-shirt back on. That's when Stella emerged from the bathroom.

"I've got to go," I said.

"You don't have to," she replied, but she was too shot up to pose any serious resistance.

"Stop smirking," I said to the kid in the hallway, and left the building.

It took all I had to beat my way through the sandstorm back to Joyce's. Every bit of me was full of sand, which chafed my face. Joyce was lying in bed under the ceiling fan, with a big wet kerchief draping her face. I showered and lay down beside her.

"Do you believe in ghosts?" I asked.

"Sure I do."

"Even that they haunt people?"

"Yes. Don't you die, M'zungu."

"Did you see your kid's ghost, too?"

"No, M'zungu. Only the living have ghosts."

"I don't believe in ghosts," I said.

"They haunt all the same."

"Uh-huh."

"You've got to do something with it."

"Why?"

"Because if you don't, it will eat you up alive."

"What do you mean by that?"

"That you'll die from it, M'zungu. That's what."

I'd been living at Joyce's place for a month already. I'd made myself at home. I'd gotten used to everything and everyone. The child's ghost alone reminded me that once I'd had another life. I didn't bother with it.

I even managed to remedy the insomnia. Though I couldn't sleep more than four hours a day, at least the four hours was certain. When sleepless nights started piling up all the same, I always held an opium day.

For that, I had a special little ritual.

I'd bought an opium pipe in the City of the Dead. A sixteen-inch, carved, ebony pipe. Its head, ornamented with floral patterns, could be screwed off. Where the head met the stem, there was a second filter. In contrast with raw opium, which the body absorbs slowly, opium smoked from a pipe takes effect immediately. The moment its breath reaches the lungs, it yanks its user into a deep vortex, down among visceral dreams. But these dreams don't last longer than ten or fifteen minutes. To again descend into the deep, you've got to relight the pipe. Which is why smoking opium is generally a group activity. If all goes well, there will be someone beside you to light the pipe when the dream kicks you out.

There was no one beside me. Though I could have asked one of the girls to help, I wasn't yearning for company. I just wanted to sleep. Besides, the girls were busy getting ready for the night.

Lighting up a second time requires superhuman effort. From the depths of opium's waves you bob up on the surface, and the air you've sucked in burns your lungs. Your limbs are stiff and numb. Moving hurts, and yet move you must, if you want to submerge again into the deep.

I worked out the ritual so as to avoid the hell of awakening. There was nothing out of the ordinary about it. I forced myself to stay awake at least until the second drag, thus ensuring myself a longer sleep after that.

Sitting in a reed armchair by the window in Joyce's room, I took the pipe in my hands, added the cooked opium paste, leaned back, and lit up. The window looked out onto the rocky desert. I stared out at the quivering air above the paved road and the filthy, weather-beaten Mercedes stationwagons rolling on by, toward el Arish, in North Sinai. The scarves of the Bedouin drivers hung out of the rolled-down windows of the cars.

The opium I'd smoked was beginning to take effect, I knew. The cars were moving ever more slowly. I started getting cold, and I had to grip the pipe tight to keep it from falling out of my hands. The tight nerves that had kept their stranglehold on me everywhere for a year let up. The angel stood behind me, pressed its finger to the nape of my neck, and let out a breath. I relit the pipe before completely stepping over into dreams. Thus it was that I managed to get a few restful hours of sleep.

The trouble occurred in the course of one of these rituals.

It was one in the morning, and there were two customers in the house. Joyce and the other two girls, who didn't have work at the moment, were already sitting in the kitchen. They were waiting for the day to end. They were drinking beer and were tired. I'd just awoken from an opium dream when I heard screaming and clattering from downstairs. I rose from the armchair and began heading half-blindly down the stairs. Opposite the front door stood a half-naked man with a knife in his hand. He was frothing from alcohol. Yaya lay on the floor in front of him. She was holding her face, and blood was flowing out from between her hands.

"I cut the thieving slut," the man shouted. Everyone had emerged to see what was happening. I continued down the stairs so I could at least go up to him, but my legs were weak. After two steps I collapsed and fainted.

I came to in the same position. My head was spinning. I stood. I heard noises from the kitchen and went there. Everyone was sitting inside. Mina was using a scarf to wash the blood from Yaya's face, which bore a six-inch gash. Yaya was crying while Mina washed her wound.

"What will become of me now?"

Except for Joyce, all the girls cast me venomous stares when I stepped into the kitchen.

"Here's our heroic rescuer," said Mina.

"Where is the man?" I asked.

"He left," said Joyce. "He got his money back and left."

"Like I said, having a white man in the house brings bad luck," said Mina.

"Stop it already," said Joyce.

"It would be better if he left. He's no use."

"I'll decide that."

"If you send Yaya away, then send this M'zungu, too."

"It's late. Everyone go to sleep."

The women stood, and each went to her room. Mina helped Yaya to bed.

Joyce and I turned in, too.

We could hear Yaya sobbing all night.

"Maybe I really should leave," I said to Joyce in bed.

"Maybe. Don't you die, M'zungu."

The next day a doctor had to be called to Yaya to stitch up her face. Joyce sent everyone away. She alone spoke with the doctor; she paid him. Tension was in the air all over the house, but no one said a thing. Even the ghost was silent. That there was serious trouble was evident from the fact that the girls did not go out to work, but instead sat silently in the kitchen, drinking beer.

Joyce was also in a bad mood. She tossed and turned in bed, and squeezed my hand in her sleep.

The situation came to a head on the morning of the third day. Joyce was no longer in the room when I awoke. Noises filtered up from downstairs. I rose from bed, got on my shirt, and went out to the staircase and looked down. Yaya was in the doorway, two big, fake Chinese Gucci suitcases beside her. A white bandage on her face. Her tears were flowing, drenching her face.

"Please, Joyce," she pleaded, "let me stay."

"You can't work."

"But soon I'll be able to."

"What will you pay the rent with in the meantime?"

"I don't know; I'll figure it out."

"I gave you enough money to get by."

"Yes. You're generous. But please don't make me leave all the same."

"You've got a place to go."

"I don't want to go."

"But I want you to go."

"Please let me stay."

"No."

"I'll do anything."

"You can't do a thing. You have to leave."

Yaya stopped crying, wiped her face, and headed outside. She shut the door behind her. For a while she stood about in front of the entrance; I could see her silhouette through the window. Finally she left.

I went down to the kitchen. Mina was sitting there, drinking a coffee.

"Only a white man has the nerve to stay after all this," she said.

I poured myself some coffee and went back to the room.

Joyce was no longer there. She'd gone into the city to tend to matters. I sat down before the window in the armchair. I stared out at the cars passing by and at the Sudanese fruit-sellers lolling about in the shade of Chinese parasols, and then decided to return to Europe. I had to wait until Joyce's return to share my decision with someone. The girls were asleep or in the city. As for the ghost, it had left without a trace.

Joyce got back in the late afternoon. Without a word she came into the room and undressed. Her enormous body was moist with perspiration.

"I'm leaving," I said.

"You don't have to leave, M'zungu."

"But I want to leave."

"Well then, go," she said, sitting down on the bed and starting to massage her feet.

I sat down beside her. Silence.

"I need a thousand dollars. When I get to Europe, I'll send it back."

A thousand dollars is a great deal of money in Egypt.

"I don't have money."

"I know you have money."

Joyce's face twisted up. Her nostrils widened, and she began to sob. She reached inside her bra and pulled out the wad of cash. It was bound with a hair tie and was moist from her sweat.

"Will you give it back?"

"Yes."

"Sure? When?"

"In a couple of days."

She removed the hair tie and unfolded the money. She divided the geneihs and the dollars. With every single dollar banknote she touched her forehead before putting it into my hand. She meanwhile cried.

"Thank you."

"Don't you die, M'zungu."

I stepped out of the currency exchange office. The September sun stung my eyes. Southern England was still hot and was cooling slowly. There wasn't a trace yet of autumn. The cafés were full of people having their lunches on terraces and sipping coffee in the shade of plane trees. As I walked down to Piccadilly Circus, I typed the transaction code into my phone. I transferred one thousand two hundred dollars back to Joyce. What with the sum I'd spent on the lawyer, practically all my money was now gone.

I sat down at a table in a pub. For a while I stared at the salt and pepper shakers and the napkin holder in front of me. The server appeared. I ordered a coffee. My phone rang, and though at first I didn't even recognize the ringtone, I then answered.

"Where are you?" said Petra.

"In the Queen's Head."

"I'm here on the corner."

"Okay."

A few breaths later in stepped the woman at whose place I'd spent the previous night. Her dress and hair were exquisite. She sat down across from me. I moved to offer her a cigarette when it struck me that smoking in taverns was no longer allowed on this continent. She smiled at the gesture.

"What will you have to drink?" I asked.

"A cappuccino."

The server appeared again, took the order, and soon delivered our coffees, which we stirred in silence.

"Thank you for letting me sleep at your place yesterday," I said.

"It's really nothing."

"Aren't you hungover? We had an awful lot to drink last night."

"No."

"I don't remember how we wound up at your place."

"I do."

"It's good you were around."

"A little angel protects the drunk," she said.

Her laughter jingled.

I looked at my phone.

I'd received a text message. Joyce had acknowledged receipt of the money.

"Now you can die, M'zungu."

Someone Is Keeping Vigil for You

"Can I smoke?" I asked, and sat down in the armchair opposite the desk. I looked around the office. Hanging on the walls, in black frames, were reprints of Chagall paintings, and behind the desk was a bookcase filled mostly with psychological texts. In the corner, a leather couch, presumably for patients. A lamp filled the room with warm, yellow light.

"Why do you want to smoke?" the woman asked. She was sitting across from me in a brown skirt and white blouse. We must have been about the same age.

"I can endure anything as long as I can smoke meanwhile."

The woman smiled and pulled out an index card with my name printed on it.

"I'm sorry, this is a nonsmoking institution."

I took out my cell phone.

"I'd like to ask you to put that away, too."

"How long will this last?"

"That's up to you."

I put the phone back in my pocket. We were silent. I tried making out the titles of the books on the shelves behind her. For quite a while I stared at the spine of the 5th edition of the *Diagnostic and Statistical Manual of Mental Disorders.*

"What are you thinking about now?"

"About fucking a psychiatrist on her office desk."

"You can't provoke me."

"Too bad."

After a few seconds of silence, the woman began again.

"Tell me about your work."

"What do you want to know?"

"What was the most violent event you saw?"

"There's lots to choose from."

"What's the first thing that comes to mind?"

"One time I saw a man in Cairo who'd been shot in the balls. He bled to death in front of me."

"Why does that come to mind?"

"I figure it touches a raw nerve."

"Did you know the man?"

"No. Because of his being shot in the balls, I mean."

"What did you feel then?"

"Hunger."

"What did you do?"

"Took pictures."

"And afterward?"

"I got something to eat."

"Mm-hmm," said the woman as she jotted something in the notebook before her and then leaned back in her chair.

"Tell me about your dreams."

"I don't have dreams."

"According to your editor, you have trouble sleeping. Insomnia or nightmares are classic symptoms of PTSD."

"I don't have PTSD."

"How do you know that? Do you even know what PTSD is?"

"I know. But you'll tell me, anyway."

"That's right. I'll tell you. Post-traumatic stress disorder, or PTSD, is an anxiety disorder that develops after a psychologically traumatic event. It qualifies as acute when its symptoms persist for three months or less, and chronic if they last for three months or more. Delayed PTSD occurs when the symptoms begin at least six months after the trauma. Did you take any medications for the insomnia?"

"All sorts."

"Since when?"

"About two years."

"And don't you feel you could use help?"

"I don't."

"You do understand that whether your contract is extended depends on my evaluation?"

"What do you want? For me to talk about how my father beat me?"

"Did your father beat you?"

"Hell he did."

"If you don't cooperate, you will lose your work."

"Then I'll apply with another agency. I don't know if you read the news, but business is booming. There are wars everywhere. They need people like me."

"Provided you can do your job."

"There was never any problem with me."

"You once hit one of your editors."

"That was a personal matter unrelated to work."

"Why did you do it?"

"Over a woman."

"Do you have a woman in your life?"

"Women, yes."

Again she jotted something in the folder.

"If you don't want to talk about your personal life, we can talk about insomnia."

"Let's."

"What is the longest you were awake?"

"One hundred twenty hours."

"Then you were already hallucinating."

"Yes."

"Do you remember?"

"No."

"How did you finally manage to sleep?"

"With Xanax and opium. Depends."

"Do you use them nowadays?"

"No."

"But you still don't have dreams."

"No. But maybe I just don't remember them."

"How much are you able to sleep a day?"

"I'll do with four hours."

The woman stood up.

"Look, I'm not here to pick on you."

"No?"

"No. I'd like to help and I propose a deal. You'll get a suitable assessment from me and you'll be able to go to Iraq, if you check into a sleep clinic for three days. You'll be subjected to nothing other than an assessment of when you sleep. After three days you'll be free to go."

"There won't be electroshock therapy or that sort of thing?"

"No. It will be about simple examinations aimed at understanding your condition."

"And regardless of your results, you'll sign the papers?"

"Yes. I promise."

"And if I don't go?"

"Then I'll write in my evaluation that you're antisocial, have drug problems, and are suffering serious PTSD."

"Do you have a beau, doctor?"

"I'm the one asking questions here."

She took her tablet from the desk drawer and began searching it.

"Will tomorrow morning do for you?"

"Yes."

She wrote something on a square slip of paper and handed it to me.

"Dr. Patrick Mitchells, somnologist, clinical psychiatrist, Early Bird Hospital," read the note, along with his institution's address in central England.

"I'll call Dr. Mitchells and arrange for them to admit you. The company is covering the costs of the examination. Are you able to travel north?"

"Yes."

"You'll be there for three days."

I stood up and left the room. I walked down the hallway and out the front door. It was a gray afternoon in London, 5 p.m. Men in dark suits were passing through the park in front of the clinic and old people sitting on benches were feeding the pigeons on the wet grass. I lit a cigarette. I walked back to the tube station and from there to my hotel.

I shuddered at the thought of having to travel to the provinces, but I was not about go looking for a new job, either. At 9 p.m. I went to the Irish pub beside the hotel and had supper. I ordered chicken wings and washed them down with four whiskeys and three mugs of beer so I could get to sleep. I woke up at 4:30 a.m.

The entrance to the grounds of Early Bird Hospital comprised an arched, wrought-iron gate. No sooner did I step in front of its electronic sensor than it opened wide. A wide gravel path led to the two-storey building, which had perhaps been some aristocratic family's manor house a century or more ago. Beside the front door was a small flower garden, which was clearly tended to daily. The grounds on each side of the building, lined with long rows of bushes, sprawled out in the wet darkness.

A short flight of steps led to the door. At the reception booth just inside was a black man in a white orderly's outfit, who smiled on seeing me.

"My name is Daniel Marosh," I said, and put my backpack on the soft-hued tile floor.

"Yes, the chief physician has been waiting for you," said the man, who emerged from the booth and headed down the hallway.

"Do follow me."

The chief physician's office was at the end of the hall. We went past a common room in which men in pajamas were sitting about and a TV was on. The receptionist knocked on the door.

"Do come in," said the chief physician.

The office was furnished in colonial style, with a large, leather couch and two armchairs, and paintings on the wall. Three people were sitting inside, each of them in a white coat. When I stepped in, everyone turned to me.

"Hello, I'm looking for Dr. Patrick Mitchells."

"That's me," replied a fortyish man with red hair and glasses.

"I am Daniel Marosh."

"The photographer Suzie told me about. Greetings."

He shook my hand.

"In a moment I'll ask one of the orderlies to show you your room."

"I can be here for three days in all."

"Then we'd best get going, no?" asked Mitchells, giving me a jovial fake punch on the side. He seemed like a good-natured fellow. I would have preferred to sock it to him right then and there.

"Meet the team. This woman here is Dr. Maggie Evans, our psychotherapist, and the gentleman is Dr. Bartlet, our somnologist."

"Hello."

I shook hands with the two doctors. The woman seemed in her early forties and was seriously overweight, and the man looked to be about my age, medium build.

"You came to the best possible place," said Dr. Evans. "We here understand those with conditions like yours."

"Insomniacs?"

"Yes," she boomed meaningfully. "Here, you can feel free to open up. Our institution is founded on trust. We build trust between patient and doctor."

"Why, that's terrific."

"Make yourself at home in your room," said Dr. Mitchells. "Get changed. Since we really don't have much time, we'll already attach you to the machine tonight in the sleep lab."

"A polysomnogram," Dr. Bartlet interjected on catching my eye. "It follows your pulse and your rate of breathing during sleep."

Dr. Mitchells picked up the phone and pressed a key.

"John," he said into the receiver, "would you come in and show the new patient his room?"

Within a few seconds the orderly came in, and led me up some stairs to the second floor, where the patients' rooms were. First, of course, he took away my phone. "This is a mobile-phone-free institution," said John.

My room comprised a bed and a closet. The furnishings did not exactly conjure up a hospital. As in the office downstairs, they too were colonial in style, and a watercolor painting hung on the wall. I unpacked my backpack. On a hanger in the closet I found a bathrobe with the institution's initials. That's what I got on over my boxers and T-shirt. Having tied it at the waist, I went off in search of the doctor.

Dr. Bartlet's office was right beside the common room. I had to ask one of the orderlies where to find him.

The "sleep observation room" included a bed and, beside it, a machine from which hung various electrodes and a mask. It was not nearly as frightening as I'd imagined. Dr. Bartlet happened to be adjusting something on it when I stepped in.

"Ah," he said, "the photographer. I wanted to ask you a couple of things."

"Go ahead."

"What is your weight?"

"Two hundred pounds."

Dr. Bartlet set the machine.

"Are you sleepy?"

"Not really."

"When do you usually fall asleep?"

"It varies."

"Did you use any stimulants today?"

"Nothing other than coffee and cigarettes."

I looked at my watch. It was almost 9:30 p.m.

"Make yourself comfortable. First I will attach these to you."

I lay down on the bed. I had to pull up my T-shirt so he could attach the electrodes to my chest. He attached the oxygen mask to my mouth.

Once we were set with that, Dr. Bartlet left the room.

I lay there in complete darkness.

How much time had passed, I'm not sure, but my mouth felt parched. I wanted to light a cigarette. I sat up in bed.

"Can we have a five-minute cigarette break?"

No one answered. I began removing the patches from myself. After finishing that I managed to find the door handle in the dark, and stepped out of the room. The light in the hallway bothered my eyes, and I kept squinting until I got used to it. The wall clock read 4 a.m.

I smelled cigarette smoke in the air. I went in its direction. That led me toward the dining room. A man in his late fifties sat at a table, in his pajamas. He was using a plastic cup as an ashtray. His skin was mottled with liver spots and was eerily white, and his eyes were bloodshot.

"Good evening," I said, took a cigarette from the pocket of my gown, sat down, and lit up.

"Who are you?" asked the man in a grating voice.

"Daniel Marosh," I said.

"Yeah. You're one of those kids, too, who killed, and now can't sleep."

"I didn't kill anyone."

"So you think. And you're not telling me nothing blew up beside you, that you didn't get shot at, and that your ego can't deal with being afraid of death? Poor little boy, you can't understand why anyone would have wanted to kill you, and now you're full of dread."

"You don't know shit about me, you fag."

"I'm not a fag."

"That's not what I meant. I don't have any problem with fags. I have a problem with pricks."

The old fellow laughed.

"Then would you tell me, Daniel Marosh, just what you're doing in this institution?"

"A London psychiatrist said my evaluation depends on getting myself examined."

"And do they know your problem already, Daniel Marosh?"

"I got here only today."

"Do *you* know your problem?"

"I don't have a problem. I don't sleep much. I'm not the first such person in history."

"Why don't you sleep much, Daniel Marosh?"

"I figure it comes with the work."

"You really think so, Daniel Marosh?"

"I don't know."

"Sure you know. A man knows full well why he can't sleep."

I took a drag on my cigarette.

"The clock is ticking," I said. "I don't have time."

"So you see, Daniel Marosh. Now that's an answer."

"Fuck that. Bigger pricks than me sleep through the night."

"Too bad that doesn't really help you. Do you envy them?"

"Fuck them. Fuck everything."

"Do you have a cigarette?"

The old fellow got up from the table and stretched out. He picked up the plastic cup and then put it back on the table. I reached into my pocket and offered him a cigarette.

"Do you believe in the soul, Daniel Marosh?" the old fellow asked, taking a drag on the cigarette.

"Not really."

"With that, you're already on the same page as Dr. Mitchells. He, too, thinks people are made up of biochemical processes, consciousness, and a nervous system."

"Yes. That's also what I think."

"Then there's nothing to fret about. You'll be cured."

"And if I don't want to be cured?"

"Why wouldn't you want to be cured? People don't like being sick."

"My not sleeping much is not an illness."

I offered the old fellow another cigarette, and then we each lit up yet again. I stood up and stepped to the drink machine at the side of the dining room. It had only tea. I searched the pocket of my gown for quite a while before realizing I had no money on me. The old fellow stood, came over to me, and poured change into the machine. I took out two teas and put one of them beside him. For a while we sat there in silence, sipping the warm, lemony instant tea.

"You know what 'keeping vigil' means?" he finally asked.

"Some old custom."

"That's right. In the old days folks used to keep vigil for the dead. It was a ritual of penitence. Jesus Christ kept vigil in the Garden of Gethsemane before he was crucified. The word originally meant to 'watch over'."

"Aha," I said, downing the rest of my tea. "I'm an atheist. Are you the camp chaplain here?"

"Are you keeping vigil for something, Daniel Marosh?"

"Then at least all this would mean something, huh?"

"You're keeping vigil for nothing."

The old fellow spoke that last sentence not so much to me, but just mumbled it to himself while staring out the window.

The sun was rising. At first it only loomed faintly in the sky, but then the black sky turned dim, and the dim sky became daybreak. Finally the sun lit up the room.

While taking my shower I wavered a bit: could I get through the next couple of days with a stone face? I concluded that I'd been in much shittier places in my life. On finishing, I returned to the dining room. The other patients were having breakfast at the tables—a bunch of twenty-something guys and a couple of middle-aged men. The old fellow was sitting alone in a corner. I took a tray—the breakfast was already on it—and sat down beside him.

"Will you have your orange juice?" he asked.

"No," I said, and handed him the juice box. He stuck in the straw and slurped the juice down loudly. The same black orderly who'd let me into the institution a day earlier now stepped to our table.

"Richard, I've already told you there's no smoking in the building."

"Sue me, John."

"Don't be smart with me, you old scoundrel, or else I won't bring you more cigarettes. Besides, you shouldn't be smoking in your condition."

He turned to me.

"The chief doctor asked that I let you know to take part in the group therapy, and then you'll have some respiratory stress tests. The doctor leading the group therapy will summon you."

"Fine."

I tried eating something but didn't really have an appetite. Before long a rotund woman—this was Dr. Evans—billowed into the dining room.

"Good morning, gentlemen. When you're done with breakfast we will meet in Room A2 and have our tea during therapy. I'd ask the new arrivals to also join us." She then left the room.

Several people got up from the tables and followed her. I stuffed half a croissant down my throat, stood up, and headed after the others.

Chairs were arranged in a semicircle in front of a table in Room A2. On the table was a red thermos, plastic cups, and a tray of biscuits. Dr. Evans was sitting beside the table with a smile. Four patients were in the room when I entered. I couldn't stare about for long, since right after me the other two newcomers arrived.

Once everyone had taken a seat, Dr. Evans began describing the aim of group therapy. I looked over the faces of the other patients. I would have bet my life that most of them were already under medication. I was surrounded by blank expressions.

"Since we have new friends in the group, I'd ask everyone to introduce himself," said Dr. Evans, not letting up on her smile for even a moment. "We'll proceed counterclockwise." I would be the sixth up.

"Let's begin," said the doctor.

First came a clean-shaven young man with black hair.

"I'm John Lewis, and I have PTSD."

"Thank you, John," said Dr. Evans. "I know you have your tea without sugar." The doctor picked up a plastic cup, pressed a serving of tea into it from the thermos, and set the cup back on the table. John then got up, took the tea and a few biscuits, and sat back down.

An older, fortyish character followed him.

"I'm Mick Stanton. My family and I had an accident, and ever since I haven't been able to sleep."

"You're very brave to face up to the past, Mick. With two sugars, right?"

From beside the table the doctor now produced a porcelain cup containing packs of sugar and plastic spoons.

Mick leaned forward, and she handed him two packs of sugar and a spoon to go with his tea.

Next came the third patient. A young, twentyish, blond kid with a frightened expression. He was anxiously rocking back and forth in his chair.

"You're next," said Dr. Evans. "What again is your name, young man?" The doctor raised the file folder that had been in her lap until now and opened it. "Jack."

"I saw the burnt-out city of madness. I walked its black streets."

"Well now, that is interesting indeed," replied Dr. Evans, still smiling. "How will you have your tea?"

"With two sugars."

"Do you want biscuits?"

"Yes."

I got up from my chair to head out. Just as I reached the door I heard the rustle of papers in the doctor's hands.

"The therapy isn't yet over, Mr. Marosh. You haven't said a thing about yourself."

"I also have my tea with two sugars."

With quick steps I went down the hallway toward the exit. I took a cigarette and lighter from the pocket of my gown and told the receptionist that I was going out for a smoke. As I stepped out the door, the wind struck my face. I lit the cigarette.

"I see that group therapy wasn't quite to your liking," came a voice to my right. Dr. Mitchells was sitting on a bench, smoking. This must have been the designated smoking place, since a large, freestanding ashtray stood by each end of the bench. I was mulling what to say in reply, but the chief doctor beat me to it.

"No need to force it. It really does help lots of people, though. Won't you sit down?"

I sat down beside him on the bench.

"John said you got to know Ronald."

"The crazy old fellow from the dining room."

"His condition really is getting worse, but I would not call him crazy."

"What's wrong with him?"

"We don't know exactly. Which is to say, we have our suspicions, but that hasn't helped us much. Ronald appears to suffer from a rare illness called fatal familial insomnia. We've ruled out nearly everything else, and I myself am completely certain that that's his illness. The symptoms include hallucinations and paranoia."

"Why isn't it treated?"

"There is no known cure for fatal familial insomnia, given that it is an inherited, prion disease. A protein has mutated in his brain, and it continuously stimulates the brain and prevents the theta waves of deep sleep, so Ronald gets no further even in sleep than the relaxed wakefulness characterized by alpha waves."

"What does that mean?"

"He can't sleep. Ever. The disease is so rare that just a handful of people in history have been diagnosed with it. It is fatal in 100 percent of cases."

"If he can't sleep, why is he still alive? I read that a person can live at most for a week without sleep, and then he'll die."

"The disease activates at a certain age. The patient slowly, over a number of years reaches the stage at which he can't sleep at all. I'm afraid that this has now occurred in Ronald's case, just as earlier in his father's."

"His father died of this disease?"

"Yes. And when the disease had Ronald in its grips and he was no longer able to care for himself, he left his entire estate to African orphans, I think."

"Did your clinic accept Ronald as a patient out of charity?"

"I was Ronald's student. What I know about somnology, I learned from him. I owe him this much. Come on now, let's go in, because you'll catch a cold. I believe you have a stress test this afternoon."

The hallway clock read 4:30 a.m. when I left the sleep lab. The light was again on in the dining room, and I smelled cigarette smoke. Ronald Helms was sitting at one of the tables, holding an English translation of *Crime and Punishment*. Beside his left hand was a paper cup he was using as an ashtray. He looked up from the book when I stepped in.

"I hear you upset Dr. Evans."

"I heard that you're going to die."

I sat down across from him and lit a cigarette. He put down the book.

"So Patrick thinks you'll persuade me that another coma will help me."

"He didn't ask for any such thing."

"But that's what he wants."

"It didn't seem like he wanted anything at all."

"Pay attention. He wouldn't have said a thing to you about me if he didn't want something."

I was silent. He continued reading.

"If you're really dying, why do you reject treatment?"

"Why do you?"

"I'm not sick."

"Nor am I."

"According to Mitchells, you will die."

"Yes, that is rather likely."

"And then?"

"No treatment will help my condition."

"Why not?"

"If I tell you, you'll think I'm crazy, just as Mitchells and everyone else in this bloody institution does."

"I already think you're crazy."

"Now that's different."

He rose from the table, stepped to the drink machine, poured in some change, pressed a button, and returned with two teas, placing one before me.

"Do you believe in curses, Daniel Marosh?"

"No. I've tried them in vain. No one died."

"My father didn't believe in them, either. For that matter, he didn't exactly believe in the Hippocratic Oath, either. When he finished university in the fifties, at first he couldn't get a job anywhere. He then became director of the clinical department of a pharmaceutical factory. From 1957 to 1960 he worked in Zimbabwe, as the chief physician for testing at the hospital in a village called Mbuma. There he met my mother, who was a nurse. I was born in 1961, in London."

"What does this have to do with your dying?"

"Don't rush me. As I said, I was born back in England. We lived a normal family life, in Gypsy Hill. Both my parents worked in the same laboratory. As regards my death, nothing noteworthy happened all the way until May 5, 1969. That's when that black man came to our house."

"Black man?"

"Nganga was his name, as I only later figured out. A witch doctor with the Shona tribe. My parents were unwilling to talk about what had happened back in Africa. By the time my father finally did, it was already way too late."

"So then, a witch doctor arrived at your place straight from Africa."

"Yes. I remember clearly. I was nine years old. It was afternoon when the doorbell rang. I went to answer it, since I thought it was Tom, the neighbor boy. Well, it wasn't Tom. A fiftyish black man stood in the door wearing a striped black wool suit and a bowler hat. His eyes were surrounded by big white stripes of paint. On seeing me, he flashed his teeth. They were gold. He asked, 'Is this where the Helms family lives?'"

"What did he want?"

"He just stood there, looking at me. I couldn't say a word. After a while my father came down the stairs, too. When he saw this black man, he went pale. He said to me, 'Come back inside, Ronnie.' I was numb; I couldn't even move."

"'What is it you want?' my father asked the man."

"'I bring greetings from the women of Mbuma and their yet unborn children,' said the man, who then lit a cigarette and blew the smoke at us. 'Since you took away our dreams, now we will take yours.'"

The old fellow lit the cigarette he'd been crinkling in his hand.

"My father told him to go to hell. Not as if it took much doing to persuade him to leave, since he went on his own, having said what he'd wanted to say."

"And this is why you're dying?"

"Not exactly. Even my great-grandfather had been a doctor. I myself was enrolled in medical school in London when my father got sick. It began with poor sleep. At first he couldn't sleep through the night. He took sleeping pills but they didn't help. He got fewer and fewer hours of sleep each night, and three years later he barely got an hour. Of course he went from one examination to another, but back then somnology had not even come to the point of effectively diagnosing fatal insomnia. My father died in 1990. On his final night, he summoned me to his bedside and, in the presence of my mother, who'd been there already and was seeking in vain to keep him from such talk, he declared that the witchdoctor was standing by his bed and whispering. He'd been seeing him there in his final days. My father had been having constant fits of rage."

"So this is why you became a psychiatrist?"

"Yes, among other reasons. I devoted all my energy to understanding what it was that had killed my father. Since the subject had a dearth of researchers, soon I was an expert."

"And what conclusion did you reach?"

"Nothing. Not even when the symptoms began emerging in my mother. She was ten years younger than my father; she fell ill later. By then I was a practicing somnologist, a clinical psychiatrist, but I could do nothing to save her. I kept trying various medicines, but not one did a thing. It was in the third year of her illness that my mother also began seeing the witchdoctor. She was convinced that she'd been cursed. One night I was at her bedside when she told me why. The pharmaceutical firm that had worked with my father in Africa had tested a new contraceptive on the people there. Since modern-day Zimbabwe did not even yet exist, the chaotic political situation allowed for this sort of thing; it was a matter of money. So then, on May 5, 1960, my father and his team tested the new serum on three hundred women—a village's entire population of women of child-bearing age. Since the serum had seen good test results in previous, animal experiments, not for a moment did they imagine that such problems would arise. All three hundred women died of internal bleeding within a week."

"I suppose that as per proper, colonialist custom no one was ever held responsible."

"Of course not. My parents returned to England and the matter was swept under the rug, with no one held to blame. After all, who would have represented an African village in an international court?"

"Well, that witchdoctor, for example."

"My mother was convinced that she was dying on account of the witchdoctor. She wanted to find him and clarify the situation, to pay him off or otherwise settle the matter."

"From London?"

"No. We traveled to Zimbabwe and went to the hospital building where the women had been killed."

"I assume you found nothing there."

"Only the hospital walls were left, and everything was overgrown with weeds. We made inquiries at nearby villages. They nearly lynched us on learning who we were."

"And?"

"They saw that my mother was dying, so they left her alone. When we asked the survivors about the witchdoctor, they couldn't say who it was. They said that they hadn't sent any curse."

"Interesting."

"Yes. After we returned to London, I did a bit of research. Three people in all from that village had gone to Europe. Two women and one man. The man was called Patrice, and he'd wound up in England with the help of foundations."

"He was the witchdoctor?"

"Yes, though by the time I identified him, I could no longer show his picture to my mother, since she died."

"You talked to him?"

"No. Patrice N'botu has been dead for years. He died in a car accident as an old man. Those who'd known him said he'd been obsessed with that drug testing, that he sought by any means to bring those responsible to justice. But the authorities were uninterested in a decade-old crime with no evidence.

"That's too bad."

"You're telling me. I tried figuring out what could be done with this type of insomnia. I prepared case studies, I practiced medicine. Then I, too, began to see the witchdoctor. I tried explaining the situation to colleagues, but they all thought I was hallucinating on account of the insomnia."

"You see him now, too?"

"Yes. He's sitting beside you."

"What is he doing?"

"Laughing."

"I thought you can't stay awake for years."

"You can't. This, however, is a unique condition. The alpha waves characterizing the relaxation necessary to drift off to sleep and are essential to the normal working of the brain don't cease all at once—but steadily over a long period of time, until they finally vanish altogether. I figure I still have about thirty minutes a day, hence I still have six months left."

"Have you seen other such cases?"

"Aside from my parents? No. Cases have been described in the literature, however, though even the diagnosis itself has existed only since the middle of the twentieth century."

"Mitchells said you were an exceptional psychotherapist."

"Oh, yes. I believe I counted as one of the foremost experts in post-traumatic stress disorder until I went mad. My success rate was outstanding and I earned a great deal of money. For example, I had a patient who was an Iraq War veteran tormented by terrible nightmares. The poor wretch begged me to take away his dreams. He said, 'Doctor, take away these dreams. I don't want to dream at all.' He didn't let go of my hand until I said to him, 'Alright, I'll take them away.' The next day he showed up at therapy with gratitude, having slept well."

"I never heard of such a thing."

"Nor had I. And yet it worked with others, too. With more than 200 patients. Of course I had to maintain the appearance of the scientific rigmarole. I got a couch for my office and over the course of four or five months each I listened to the grateful patients' crap, for an hourly fee of one hundred pounds. I tried finding an explanation. It seems this was a side-effect of the curse. I was able to take away other people's bad dreams, because my punishment was keeping vigil."

"Or else you have delusions on account of the insomnia."

"Or that. And yet I have the boundless gratitude of 200 people and their families. I had to open a separate folder on my computer for the thank-you letters. Do you have bad dreams?"

"No, I don't. I dream of angels who breathe whipped cream."

"Then what are you doing here?"

"I don't sleep much."

"Do you want me to take away your dreams?"

"I wouldn't want to burden you with my problems for all the world. You're crazy enough as it is."

"One more or one less, it's all the same."

"Like I said, I have no nightmares."

"Believe me, it's much easier if someone keeps vigil for you. Most of us die because no one does so for us. I'll keep vigil for you, Daniel Marosh."

"Well, that's terrific."

"Take my hand."

I took it.

"Someone is keeping vigil for you," he said. For several seconds I stared into his delirious, bloodshot eyes.

"Okay, now you can let go of my hand."

"Someone is keeping vigil for you," he repeated, and let it go. I stood up from the table.

"I'm going off to take a shower," I said.

Dawn was breaking.

Breakfast comprised croissants with plum jam. Chewing away all around me were the faces I'd seen at group therapy. The old fellow was nowhere in sight. After finishing breakfast, I knocked on the door to Mitchells's office, but no one answered.

"He's in the sleep lab," said an orderly who noticed me in front of the door.

I went over. The room was open. The old fellow was now lying on the bed I'd been on earlier. He was strapped down. An IV was attached to his right arm. He was breathing through a mask. Electrodes were patched to his chest and head, the wires running to the machine beside which stood Dr. Mitchells, who knit his brows anxiously.

"Sorry," I said.

"Mr. Marosh! Come in."

"What happened?"

"Ronald attacked John, the orderly who came for his morning shift. He had to be sedated."

"I'm sorry."

"I am, too," said Dr. Mitchells. "Take a look at this," he added, turning the monitor my way. Various readouts were jumping about on it, with symbols I couldn't understand.

"What am I looking at?"

"The readout on top shows the brain function. See how active it is."

"I see. Shouldn't it be that way?"

"No. Ronald's brain is right now working just as if he were awake and, say, was having a conversation with someone. Judging from the amount of haloperidol he was given, practically speaking he should be in a vegetative state."

"So he's not sleeping even now?"

"No."

We fell silent.

"I assume you came to check out."

"Yes."

"Come with me to my office, where you can sign the paperwork."

Mitchells sat down at his desk and I sat across from him.

"Your test results are in," he said.

"And what is my problem?"

"You suffer from sleep apnea."

"What does that mean?"

"Your breathing stops in the deep sleep stage, causing you to wake up."

"I understand. And is this dangerous?"

"Persistent insomnia is. You should make changes to your diet, you should quit smoking, and you should avoid stress. All those factors can induce it."

"I see. Where do I sign?"

"Here is your discharge form," he said, sliding a paper across the desk. I signed it.

"There are also medications that could help with sleep. I sent the information to your psychiatrist in London. Sure you can't stay longer? There would be a few more tests we'd need to perform."

"Sure."

"Well then, glad to have made your acquaintance."

I arrived in London at 4 p.m. After checking in at the hotel, I turned on my laptop. Among my emails, there was the doctor's "satisfactory" evaluation and a private message in which she asked me to phone her before returning to the Middle East. On getting the good news, I opened the minibar and downed two little bottles of Jack Daniels. Then I went out to Hyde Park and sat about on a bench.

Once it began getting dark, I stood up and went to the same Irish bar I'd been in a few days earlier. I had dinner, but I was not in the mood for the crowd that flooded in for the 9 p.m. match on the TV. By 9:30 I was back in my room, plugged my phone in to charge, and sprawled out on the bed.

I slept like a baby.

Crow Soup

The mist was rising from the freshly plowed farmland. The fog lights of the Ford Focus illuminated the bare trees bordering the fields. There was no traffic on the road. Kristóf's dad gripped the steering wheel with both hands. He was anxious. He waited for the man's silhouette to finally appear by the side of the road. More than once he raised a cigarette to his mouth, but he always returned it to its pack when he reached to pull down the window. He didn't want to let the early morning wind into the car, which was warm from breathing.

Kristóf saw nothing of daybreak. He was asleep, curled up on the back seat under a striped blue blanket, his hands tucked under his head as a makeshift pillow. His father often looked back to be sure the kid didn't push the blanket off himself. The little boy sometimes stirred and mumbled something in his sleep.

It was a cool, early spring day. They were just 6 kilometers from Vitnyéd, a village on the plains of western Hungary.

The time on the dashboard above the radio read 5 a.m. The cell phone rang. Taking his right hand off the steering wheel, Kristóf's dad reached into the pocket of his jacket on the passenger seat.

"We'll be there soon," he said into the phone.

"Where are we going?" came Kristóf's voice from the back seat.

His dad glanced into the rearview mirror. The kid was with him for three days, on a parental visitation.

"We're going to visit an old lady," he replied.

"What lady?"

"A lady who's very sick."

"Why is the lady sick?"

"Because she's old," said Kristóf's dad.

"I don't like old people."

"Compared to you I'm old, too. The lady we're going to visit is like a second mother to me."

A man's silhouette loomed on the right side of the road, just beside the sign that read, "Vitynéd." Kristóf's dad slowed, stopped, and got out of the car. Kristóf watched through the window as his dad stepped over to the figure outside. For a couple of seconds the two men just stood there, staring at each other with bemused expressions, but then they hugged and together returned to the car. Kristóf's dad opened the door and removed his jacket from the passenger seat. The other man got in. Only now could Kristóf get a closer look at him. He was a large, dark-skinned man, in a scuffed leather jacket and a checkered flannel shirt.

"This is Kristóf, my son," said Kristóf's dad to the man. Turning back, he now said to his son, "This is Uncle Laci, your dad's friend."

"Feel free to call me Laci, Kristóf," said the man, extending his hand to the boy. He had deep-set, jittery, brown eyes. Kristóf shook his hand in fear. They drove on.

"I'll let you know where we have to turn," said Laci.

"Okay."

"You look good. How long has it been since we last saw each other? Ten years?"

"More like fifteen. How's Aunt Kuki, your mom?"

"The doctor let her home from the hospital. Not because she's better. Mother isn't good at all. That's also why we got in touch."

"It's good you did."

"I'm glad you could come. That both of you could."

"Of course."

"Did you bring the rifle?"

"Yes. It's in the trunk."

"Good, then."

Huddled into the corner of the back, Kristóf stared with suspicion at the stranger. Finally he spoke up.

"Uncle Laci, why is your skin so dark?"

"Kristóf," growled his dad.

Laci's face lit up.

"Because I'm a Gypsy, my son," he said, turning back and giving the boy's leg a pat. "And Gypsies have darker skin."

"This is where we should have turned."

Kristóf's dad braked and backed up. The reverse lights colored the fog red. They reached the turnoff, a dirt road. Turning onto it, the car began to shake as they moved forward slowly. Finally, the contours of a little peasant house came into view right by the woods. The house was surrounded by a big, rusty iron fence, with several cars out front in the yard, which was unkempt, with heaps of scrap metal on the packed earth. The baying of dogs could be heard coming from the open windows of the house.

"I'll go tie up the dogs," said Laci and got out of the car.

"Listen, Kristóf, I'd like it if you were very nice to the people here," said Kristóf's dad.

"Okay."

"You know, the lady we've come to see helped out your grandmother a whole lot."

"How did she help?"

"When I was born, you know, I was in big, big trouble."

"As big trouble as I was in?"

"Even bigger. Csufi, your grandmother, my mother, was a really, really little gal, not much heavier than a feather. She almost died giving me birth. The doctors fought for days to save her life."

"And this lady saved Csufi's life?"

"No, my son. It was my life that Aunt Kuki saved. You see, Csufi was so weak that she couldn't even feed me. Aunt Kuki fed me instead. I was still a little baby. You know what little babies eat?"

"Yes. Milk. From their mommies' boobies."

"Just like you did. It was Aunt Kuki who fed me when I was a little baby."

They got out of the car and headed toward the house.

Laci was waiting for them by the front gate. The dogs were still baying, but now from further off. The hubbub of children at play filtered their way from the yard. Kristóf and his father looked, and saw five little kids scampering about outside in the shadow of the scrap metal.

"This way," said Laci.

He led Kristóf and his father through the yard and into the house. The scent of wax mixed with that of clothing inside. Candles were burning. The lighting was dim. Eight people were sitting in the largest room of the peasant house. Four men and four women. The men were all wearing white shirts and black suit coats; the women, black skirts with floral embroideries, and had kerchiefs on their heads. In the middle of the room was a wood-framed double bed. A scrawny old woman with a furrowed face lay among the quilts. She was in a skirt and a red blouse. Her face was rouged and lipstick shone on her lips. Beside the bed was an IV pole, and the tube led to her left arm. The woman was unconscious.

"They're here," said Laci on stepping into the room.

"Hi everyone," said Kristóf's dad.

Kristóf spontaneously took his father's hand.

"Hi," said a thirtyish woman. Kristóf's dad now recognized her as Kuki's daughter, Ágnes. They'd played together for years as children. Her eyes were red from crying, like those of the other women.

"Thank you for coming."

"Of course, Ági."

"Is he your son?"

"Yes."

"He's just like you were," said Ágnes. "Come on, little boy, you must be hungry. Let me give you a nice thick slice of fresh bread with lard and salt on top."

"I don't like bread with lard," Kristóf replied and hid behind his father's leg. His dad leaned down to his son.

"Dad's got to talk over a couple of things. If you're not hungry, go out and play with the kids in the yard, Okay?"

"Okay."

Kristóf headed toward the yard. His dad watched him disappear down the hallway. On hearing the door to the yard slam shut, he turned again to the adults. He looked at the rawboned old woman on the bed and could not reconcile her with his memory of the large, vibrant woman who had been a constant guest in their home in his early years.

"How is she?"

"Yesterday she was awake for only an hour," said Ágnes. "The doctor said she'd pass today." She fell to tears.

The other women began crying, too. Kristóf's dad sat down on one of the chairs and stared straight ahead. When he looked up from his ruminations he saw his son standing by the entrance to the room in wonderment. He stood up and went over to him.

"What's the matter, Kristóf?"

"The other kids are barefoot, Dad."

"They don't want to get mud on their dress shoes. Go ahead and take off your shoes, too."

"It's cold."

"If the little girls are barefoot, too, it can't be that cold."

He caressed the boy's head and took him to the front door. He watched as Kristóf slipped lissomely out of his sneakers and removed his socks. Slowly, hesitantly he stepped out to the yard; he wasn't used to walking barefoot.

He'll get used to it, thought his dad. *I did too.*

For a while he watched his son as he went back over to the other children and joined them in play.

"You should go out," said Laci to Kristóf's dad, putting a hand on his shoulder. "May that much be accomplished, at least, since she asked for it."

"I'm going," said Kristóf's dad, and stood up.

He got on his jacket and went out to the yard. The sun had completely done away with the fog by now. The air was warmer, too. He walked to the car. He opened the trunk and took out the IZS27 shotgun. He opened the barrel to see if there was a shell in it. There wasn't. He reached into the cardboard box that had been beside the gun, took out four red shells, and stuffed them into his jacket pocket.

"Kristóf!" he called out.

His son looked up and ran over to him.

"I'm going hunting. Won't you come with me?"

"I will."

They went out to the dirt road, on each side of which moist grass was sparkling blue.

"What are we hunting, Dad?" asked Kristóf.

"Crows."

"Why are we hunting crows?"

"To eat them."

"But you can't eat crows. Only rabbits, wild boar, and deer."

"You can eat crows, too. It's just that we're not in the habit of doing so."

"Why not?"

"Because we eat crow only on really special occasions. When someone is very sick."

"And we're now hunting because the lady is very sick?"

"Yes. The Gypsies believe that death flies on a crow's wings. By eating crows they can scare it away."

For a while they walked beside each other without a word. Kristóf broke the silence.

"My feet hurt a little, Dad."

Kristóf's dad looked at the boy and only then realized he hadn't gotten on his shoes.

"Do you want me to put you on my shoulders?"

"No. I'm a big boy already. It's enough if we go more slowly."

Kristóf's dad stepped out of his own shoes and took off his socks. He tied the shoes together by the laces and slung them on his shoulder. They went on. Ten minutes later they left the dirt road and walked through the plowed field. The oleaginous black earth squelched under their weight. They went all the way to the middle of the field. They stopped on seeing a flock of crows, fat ones, some twenty meters away, clawing at the soil. Kristóf began hopping about excitedly.

"There they are, there they are," he said, pointing to the crows.

"Keep quiet. If they notice us, they'll fly off. Crows are very smart animals."

"They can't be smarter than us."

Kristóf's dad took the shotgun off his shoulder.

"Can I load it?" asked the boy.

"If you're careful."

Kristóf picked up the gun. Careful to have it pointing at the ground, he opened the barrel. He was looking at his dad the whole time. His dad handed him two of the shells. The boy stuffed them into the barrel, and then his dad snapped the barrel back in place.

"You did it well."

"I can hardly wait to shoot the gun myself," the boy whispered.

"When you're able to hold the gun more easily."

Kristóf's dad took the weapon, released the safety, and pressed the stock against his shoulder. He fired once, twice. The bang echoed off the distant trees. Several dozen crows flew up into the air.

"You got some, you got some!" yelled the boy, running over to where his dad had shot. Four birds were lying on the ground.

They got back to the house an hour later. Kristóf was riding on his dad's shoulders. His dad held the shotgun in one hand, and with his other hand he held the four crows by their feet. Blood dripped from their heads onto the dirt road. The dogs were not barking. The breeze carried snatches of singing their way from the house.

Where I wander, even the trees do weep,
Leaves are falling from its branches so weak.
Fall on down, leaves, hide me, cover me up. . . .

Kristóf's dad put down his son and opened the iron gate. Laci was standing in the yard. He was shaking from his tears. In his hand was a kitchen knife, with which he was cutting the buttons off his shirt.

"My dear mother has died," he said.

Kristóf's dad stepped into the house, his son following close behind. In the hallway the women, still singing, were turning backward the pictures and the mirror on the wall. The men, sitting, were wordlessly cutting the buttons off their suit coats. The dead woman was lying there as if asleep. Her hands had been clasped over her chest.

"I'll take that," said Ági on noticing Kristóf and his dad.

She took the crows from Kristóf's dad and went to the kitchen.

Kristóf's dad lit a cigarette in the yard.

"Did the lady die because we didn't hurry enough?" asked Kristóf.

"I don't think so. She was old and very sick."

"Will we die this way, too, Dad?"

"Not necessarily like this. But it's certain that we will."

"When I die, will you shoot crows for me?"

"Yes. I'll shoot you some crows."

"And will you hurry up doing so?"

"Yes, I'll hurry."

"I'll shoot crows for you, too."

"I know," replied the dad, caressing the boy's head. "I'm sorry. I shouldn't have brought you with me."

"What will they do now?"

"They'll mourn their mother for three days. Then they'll go back to Germany."

"Will they eat the crows?"

"Yes. That will be lunch. We don't have to wait around for that."

"I'd like to wait," said Kristóf.

The women set a plastic table in the yard. They cooked the crows in a big brown pot, and ladled out the soup into each person's bowl. The red meat alone reminded them that it wasn't chicken. Kristóf had three bowls, which surprised his dad.

After lunch they said goodbye to the whole family and got back in the car. They headed off. For twenty minutes they didn't say a word to each other. Kristóf's dad figured the boy was asleep. Only on looking into the rearview mirror did he notice that he was awake. The little boy was sitting there, his legs pulled up, worried eyes gazing out the window.

"What's the matter?"

"I'm wondering if we ate enough."

"For what?"

"To scare away death."

"We sure did," said Kristóf's dad. "Don't you worry on account of that."

Kristóf kept looking out the window. The trees were blooming by the side of the road, and the crops were sprouting on the fields. With the sparkling sunlight, too, it seemed death really was very far away.